DEAR SWEETGUM

A SWEETGUM MEADOWS ROMANCE BOOK 14

IMANI PRICE

Copyright © 2025 by Imani Price
www.ImaniPrice.com

First Edition: November 2025

ISBN 979-8-89283-317-2 (ebook)
ISBN 979-8-89283-318-9 (paperback)

Published by Books to Hook Publishing, LLC.
www.BooksToHook.com

CONTENTS

CHAPTER ONE

Danielle Jacobs stared at her computer screen, watching the cursor blink mockingly at the end of a half-finished spreadsheet. The quarterly data analysis that should have taken two hours had stretched into its fourth, thanks to a system crash that wiped out her morning's work. Around her, the hum of fluorescent lights mixed with the distant chatter of coworkers discussing weekend plans—plans that probably didn't involve pivot tables and data validation formulas.

She rubbed her temples, fighting off the familiar ache that came from staring at numbers all day. When had her life become nothing but cells and columns? When had she stopped dreaming about stories and started drowning in statistics?

The irony wasn't lost on her. She'd majored in English literature with dreams of becoming a writer, spending college nights crafting poetry and short stories that her professors praised for their emotional depth and keen observation. But student loans and practical parents had steered her toward "stable employment," and somehow stable had become synonymous with soul-crushing.

Her phone buzzed with a text from her sister Chrysta:

> Mom wants to know if you're bringing anyone to Aleeyah's anniversary dinner Sunday. I told her probably not, but she's hoping.

Heat crept up Danielle's neck. Even her family assumed she'd show up alone—again. Not that they were wrong, but the casual certainty stung. At twenty-three, she was the only Jacobs sister without a plus-one, without someone to text during boring work days, without anyone who cared if she made it home safely.

She typed back:

> Tell Mom I'm bringing my sparkling personality. That should be enough entertainment.

The response came quickly:

> Ha. Just saying, there's nothing wrong with putting yourself out there. You won't meet anyone hiding behind spreadsheets.

Danielle set her phone aside with more force than necessary. Easy for Chrysta to say—she had Terrence and their picture-perfect relationship that had blossomed from a fake engagement into real love. Easy for Aleeyah too, glowing with newlywed happiness after her fairy-tale romance with Greg. But what was the alternative? Download another dating app? Suffer through awkward coffee dates with men who talked about themselves for an hour straight?

She'd tried dating, but the results had been mixed at best. Sweetgum Meadows had its share of nice guys, but the connections just hadn't clicked. There was a guy from the hardware store, who was perfectly pleasant but spent their entire coffee date discussing his extensive collection of vintage tools. Then there was another guy who was recently divorced and still processing his feelings about his ex-wife, which made for some heavy first-date conversation. And while she appreciated the last guy's passion for outdoor activities, his enthusiasm for hunting and fishing didn't quite match her own interests.

The dating apps weren't yielding better results. Her profile attracted occasional messages, but most conversations fizzled out after a few exchanges. It seemed like everyone was looking for something—she just wasn't sure what, or if she was looking for the same thing. Maybe the problem wasn't the men she was meeting; maybe she simply hadn't figured out what kind of connection she was actually seeking.

A notification popped up on her screen—another data request from her supervisor, Patricia, who seemed to believe that the solution to every business problem lay buried somewhere in spreadsheet formulas. Danielle sighed, minimizing her personal spreadsheet to focus on work. But as she pulled up the new project, her gaze drifted to the window beside her desk.

Outside, Main Street bustled with afternoon activity. People walked with purpose, met friends for coffee, lived actual lives instead of analyzing other people's business metrics. Mrs Chen from the flower shop was arranging a sidewalk display of autumn mums. Two teenagers shared earbuds and laughed at something on their phone. An elderly couple held hands as they window-shopped, probably married for decades and still choosing each other daily.

When was the last time she'd done something spontaneous? Something just for the joy of it? She couldn't remember the last time she'd written anything creative, the last time she'd read a book for pleasure instead of collapsing into bed after ten hours of number-crunching.

Her college poetry journal sat in her apartment closet, buried under winter coats and boxes of tax documents. Sometimes she caught herself composing lines in her head during her commute, but by the time she got home, exhaustion won out over inspiration. The girl who'd once stayed up until three AM crafting the perfect metaphor had been replaced by someone whose greatest creative achievement was finding new ways to format pivot tables.

The lunch bell chimed, and Danielle made a decision. Instead of eating her usual desk salad while reviewing reports, she grabbed her purse and headed for the door. Fresh air might help clear her head, and the walk to the library would do her good. Maybe she'd even check out a poetry collection, remember what words could do when they weren't confined to business reports.

"Taking an actual lunch break?" asked Janet from the neighboring cubicle, looking up from her own screen with surprised amusement.

"Revolutionary concept, I know," Danielle replied, pulling on her cardigan. "If Patricia asks, I'm conducting field research on work-life balance."

Main Street looked different when she wasn't rushing to or from work. The late September sun cast everything in golden light, and the trees were just beginning to hint at autumn colors. She passed the comic book store where Demetrius was setting up a sidewalk display, waved to Malakai through the window of Rochelle's diner, and felt some of her tension ease.

Sweetgum Meadows had its charms when you took time to notice them. The historic downtown had been lovingly preserved, with brick sidewalks and wrought-iron benches that invited lingering. Street art murals decorated the sides of buildings, created by local artists who captured the town's spirit in vibrant colors. It was the kind of place where people still knew their neighbors, where small businesses thrived through community support rather than corporate backing.

She'd grown up here, taken it for granted through high school, and only recently begun to appreciate the genuine connections that small-town life fostered. Maybe the problem wasn't her location—maybe the problem was that she'd stopped participating in the community that surrounded her.

The Sweetgum Library sat at the corner of Main and Oak, its brick facade covered in ivy that turned brilliant red each fall. Danielle climbed the front steps, breathing in the scent of old books and wood polish that always reminded her of childhood story hours. This place had been her sanctuary growing up, where she'd discovered Anne of Green Gables and Jane Austen, where Mrs Williams had first encouraged her love of words.

Inside, Mrs Everly Williams looked up from the circulation desk with a welcoming smile. She was in her seventies but moved with the energy of someone half her age, her silver hair perfectly styled despite spending her days reorganizing shelves and chasing down overdue books. She'd been the town librarian for as long as anyone could remember, a fixture of knowledge and kindness who somehow knew exactly what book each patron needed.

"Danielle! How lovely to see you during daylight hours." Mrs Williams set aside a stack of returned books. "Taking a proper lunch break for once?"

"Trying to." Danielle approached the desk, noting how the afternoon light streamed through the tall windows, illuminating dust motes that danced like tiny stars. "I forget how peaceful it is here."

"Libraries have that effect. Something about being surrounded by thousands of stories tends to put daily troubles in perspective." Mrs Williams gestured toward the poetry section. "Looking for anything particular, dear?"

Danielle was about to answer when her eyes caught a colorful flyer taped to the counter. "What's this about?"

Mrs Williams followed her gaze and beamed with the enthusiasm of someone who'd discovered the perfect solution to a long-standing problem. "'Dear Sweetgum'—my latest project. We're starting an anonymous pen-pal exchange program.

Participants write letters under pseudonyms, and I match them based on interests and personality. It's meant to foster authentic connections in our community."

Danielle studied the flyer more closely. The idea was elegantly simple: fill out an interest survey, choose a pen name, and be matched with another participant. All correspondence would go through the library to maintain anonymity until both parties agreed to reveal themselves.

"Anonymous?" she asked, intrigued despite herself.

"Completely. I'm the only one who knows real identities, and I'm sworn to secrecy unless someone violates the guidelines." Mrs Williams leaned forward conspiratorially. "We've had such wonderful response already. People are hungry for real conversation, meaningful dialogue. Social media gives us the illusion of communication, but where's the depth? The thoughtfulness?"

Something stirred in Danielle's chest—a flutter of possibility she hadn't felt in months. When was the last time someone had asked about her dreams, her thoughts, her actual self rather than her data analysis skills? When had she last had a conversation that went deeper than weather, work, and weekend plans?

"I've been thinking about this program for years," Mrs Williams continued, settling into what was clearly a favorite topic. "We live in an age of instant everything—instant messages, instant gratification, instant judgment. But some things can't be rushed. Real understanding takes time, patience, careful consideration of words."

She gestured toward the letter-writing station she'd set up near the reference desk, complete with quality paper, good pens, and a small collection of books about the art of correspondence.

"How does it work exactly?" Danielle found herself asking.

"You fill out this form with your interests, what you're looking for in a correspondence—friendship, intellectual discussion, creative exchange. Choose a pen name that represents how you want to be known. I match you with someone compatible based on your responses, and you start writing." Mrs Williams handed her a clipboard. "Letters only, no emails or texts. There's something magical about handwritten words, don't you think? The time it takes to form each letter, the permanence of ink on paper, the intimacy of seeing someone's actual handwriting."

Danielle took the form, scanning the questions. *What do you hope to find through this program? What would you like to share about yourself that others might not know? Describe your ideal conversation. What matters most to you in human connection?*

"I don't know," she said slowly, though her fingers were already itching to hold a pen. "What if we don't click? What if I'm boring? What if I don't have anything interesting to say?"

"My dear, you're anything but boring. You're thoughtful, intelligent, and you have stories worth telling—you just need someone who wants to hear them." Mrs Williams patted her hand with maternal warmth. "Besides, that's the beauty of anonymity. You can be exactly who you are without worrying about assumptions or social expectations. No judgment based on appearance, age, social status, or any of the superficial things that complicate face-to-face interactions."

Danielle looked at the form again. *What would you like to share about yourself that others might not know?* She thought about her abandoned creative writing dreams, her secret poetry collection, her longing for conversations that went deeper than surface pleasantries. How long had it been since she'd met someone who cared about ideas, who wanted to explore thoughts and feelings that couldn't be captured in casual small talk?

"How many people have signed up?" she asked, surprised by her own growing interest.

"Twenty-three so far, ranging from teenagers to retirees. My grandson Chris has been helping me with the logistics—he's quite excited about the literary possibilities. We have teachers, artists, business owners, students, retirees. All kinds of people looking for the same thing you are."

Twenty-three people in Sweetgum who also craved real connection. Maybe she wasn't as alone as she'd thought. Maybe there were others who felt like they were sleepwalking through their days, going through the motions of living without really engaging with life.

"What kind of pen name should I choose?" The question surprised her with its seriousness. Somehow this felt important, like choosing how she wanted to be known in some essential way.

Mrs Williams smiled knowingly. "Something that captures who you want to be in these letters. Your authentic self, perhaps —the person you are when no one's watching, when you're not performing any particular role."

Danielle thought about that as she found a quiet corner table to fill out the form. When no one was watching, she was someone who noticed the way morning light hit her coffee cup, who made up stories about strangers she passed on the street, who still believed in the kind of love that inspired poetry and changed lives. She was someone who saw beauty in data patterns but yearned for the messier, more meaningful patterns of human emotion and connection.

She was someone who'd once written a poem about maple trees that her college professor had called "luminous with possibility," someone who still sometimes caught herself crafting metaphors about ordinary moments.

Under "Pen Name," she wrote:

Maplewood Muse

Under "What you hope to find," she wrote:

Someone who believes words matter, who thinks deeply about small things, who won't judge my tendency to see stories everywhere. Someone interested in exploring what it means to be human in thoughtful, honest ways.

Under "What you'd like to share," she wrote:

My observations about finding beauty in unexpected places, my questions about how to live authentically, my belief that the right conversation can change everything.

She handed the clipboard back to Mrs Williams, pulse quickening with nervous excitement and something that felt dangerously close to hope.

"Excellent choice," the librarian said, reading over her responses with obvious approval. "I have a feeling Maplewood Muse is going to find exactly what she's looking for."

As Danielle walked back to work, autumn air crisp against her cheeks and possibility humming in her veins, she felt lighter than she had in weeks. For the first time in months, she was looking forward to something that had nothing to do with data analysis or family expectations. Somewhere in Sweetgum, another person was hoping for the same kind of connection she craved.

Maybe putting herself out there didn't have to mean awkward coffee dates and dating apps. Maybe it could be as simple as honest words on paper, shared between strangers who might become something more.

The afternoon spreadsheets didn't seem quite so tedious after that.

CHAPTER TWO

Darius Jones stood behind the counter of Sweetgum Bookstore, methodically cataloging a box of donated books that had arrived that morning. The familiar ritual of sorting, evaluating, and pricing helped quiet the restless energy that had been building in his chest for weeks now. Outside, the late September afternoon cast long shadows through the front windows, painting golden rectangles across the worn wooden floors and illuminating the spines of books displayed in the window like jewels waiting to be discovered.

He held up a well-worn copy of Pride and Prejudice, checking the spine for damage. The pages fell open to a passage someone had underlined in pencil: "There is nothing like staying at home for real comfort." In the margin, different handwriting had added: "But what if home feels like a cage?"

The question resonated more than he cared to admit. Three months ago, moving into the small apartment above the bookstore had felt like the perfect solution—close enough to help his aging grandparents daily, independent enough to maintain his own space and routines. He'd imagined quiet mornings spent writing, afternoons discovering local stories, evenings discussing literature with his grandfather over dinner at their house down the street.

Reality had proven more complicated. The mornings were quiet, certainly, but often filled with an emptiness that surprised him. The local stories existed, but many of the older residents who carried them seemed hesitant to share with someone they still saw as "Robert's grandson" rather than someone genuinely interested in preserving their experiences. And while his grandparents welcomed him warmly every Sunday, the rest of the week stretched with a loneliness he hadn't anticipated.

The bookstore itself reflected this contradiction. Housed in a building that had served the community for over sixty years, it contained treasures that would delight any serious reader—first editions, local histories, collections of poetry that revealed the hearts of previous owners through their marginalia. But foot traffic had declined steadily, and many days passed with only a handful of customers, mostly elderly regulars who bought the same genres week after week.

Darius had inherited the store from his great-aunt, along with her meticulous record-keeping and her belief that books were meant to be touched, read, and loved rather than displayed like museum pieces. He honored her memory by maintaining the warm, welcoming atmosphere she'd created, but some days he wondered if he was simply tending a shrine to a dying way of life.

The bell over the door chimed, and Mrs Patterson shuffled in, moving slowly with her walker. She visited every Tuesday, always bought the same romance series, always paid with exact change counted out from a small coin purse.

"Good afternoon, Mrs Patterson," Darius said warmly, setting aside the donated books. "The new Beverly Jenkins came in yesterday. I set it aside for you."

"You're such a thoughtful boy," she said, making her way to

the counter with careful steps. "Your grandparents raised you right."

Mrs Patterson had known the family for decades, remembered when this bookstore was the heart of Sweetgum's social life instead of a quiet refuge for a handful of regulars. Sometimes Darius wondered if he was watching the end of an era, cataloging the final chapter of a story that had been unfolding since before he was born.

"How's your reading group going?" he asked as he rang up her purchase.

"Oh, we're down to just four of us now. Mildred moved to live with her daughter in Savannah, and Dorothy's eyes aren't what they used to be." Mrs Patterson's smile was tinged with melancholy. "Hard to discuss books when half the group can't see the pages anymore."

The comment settled heavily in his chest. How many communities of readers were quietly dissolving, their shared love of stories scattered by time and circumstance? How many conversations about books, about ideas, about the human experience were simply... ending?

After Mrs Patterson left with her purchase and a promise to see him next Tuesday, Darius returned to the donation box. Beneath the novels, he found a stack of local history books—Sweetgum Meadows: A Century of Stories, Georgia Mill Towns in the Early 1900s, Voices from the Past: Oral Histories of Rural Georgia.

Now this was interesting. He opened the oral history book, skimming testimonials from longtime residents. These were the stories he'd hoped to discover when he moved here—authentic voices, real experiences that could breathe life into his writing. The book contained interviews conducted in the 1980s with people who'd lived through the town's cotton mill boom, the Great Depression, World War II, and the slow economic changes that had reshaped rural Georgia.

One entry caught his attention: an interview with a woman named Sarah McKenzie, who'd worked in the town's textile mill during the 1940s. She described the sense of community that had flourished among the workers, how they'd shared books, written letters to soldiers overseas, and created their own small literary society that met in the mill's break room.

"We didn't have much education, most of us," Sarah had told the interviewer, "but we had curiosity. We wanted to understand the world beyond our little town, and books were our windows. We'd read to each other during lunch breaks, discuss what we'd learned, argue about what the authors meant. Those conversations fed our souls in ways that nothing else could."

Darius set the book down, struck by the parallel between Sarah's experience and his own longing. Nearly forty years later, he was searching for the same thing—people who wanted to use books as windows, who craved conversations that fed the soul rather than simply passing time.

His phone buzzed with a text from his college roommate:

> How's small-town life treating you? Any regrets about turning down that internship at the Atlanta History Center?

Darius stared at the message, thumb hovering over the keyboard. How could he explain that some days he felt perfectly content, connected to something meaningful and lasting? And other days he felt like he was slowly disappearing, becoming as dusty and overlooked as the books on his back shelves?

The Atlanta History Center position would have meant steady income, professional development, and colleagues who shared his academic interests. It also would have meant becoming one small part of a large institution, processing other people's historical discoveries rather than making his own. Here in Sweetgum, he had the freedom to explore stories that called to him, to write without committee oversight, to build something entirely his own.

The question was whether "his own" would always mean "alone."

He typed back:

> Still settling in. Lots of character here.

It wasn't entirely a lie. Sweetgum had character—in the older residents who remembered when Main Street bustled with activity, in the younger families trying to balance tradition with progress, in the subtle rhythms of small-town life that took time to understand and appreciate. What it lacked was people his own age who understood the weight of potential unfulfilled, the pressure of choosing between security and dreams.

Most of his high school classmates had left for college and never returned, drawn to cities that offered career opportunities and cultural amenities that small towns couldn't match. The ones who stayed seemed settled in ways that both impressed and unsettled him—married young, established in family businesses, content with routines that would have felt suffocating to Darius at their age.

He envied their certainty while questioning whether it came from genuine satisfaction or simply from never having seriously considered alternatives. Were they happier because they'd found their place, or because they'd never allowed themselves to imagine other places existed?

The back door opened, and his grandmother appeared with a plate of fresh cookies and a knowing smile. At seventy-two, she moved with the confidence of someone who'd learned to find joy in small daily rituals—baking for family, tending her garden, maintaining connections with friends she'd known for decades.

"Thought you might need sustenance," she said, setting the

plate on the counter. "And to remind you about dinner Sunday. I'm making your favorite pot roast."

"Looking forward to it." He genuinely was. Sunday dinners at his grandparents' house had become the highlight of his week, a chance to connect with the people who understood him best and still believed in his dreams even when he struggled to believe in them himself.

"Your grandfather mentioned the pen-pal program at the library. Says Mrs Williams is trying to bring the community together through anonymous letter writing." His grandmother's eyes twinkled with mischief. "Might be good for someone who spends too much time alone upstairs with his notebooks."

"I'm not alone. I have customers."

"Mrs Patterson doesn't count as social interaction, dear. She's seventy-eight and mostly talks to her cats." His grandmother's voice was gentle but pointed. "You need people your own age, people who challenge you intellectually."

Despite himself, Darius smiled. His grandmother had been dropping hints about his social life—or lack thereof—since he'd moved to town. She meant well, but how could he explain that he wasn't avoiding people so much as waiting for the right people? Conversations in Sweetgum tended toward weather, local gossip, and polite inquiries about his family. What he craved was someone who wanted to dig deeper, who found ideas as interesting as individuals.

"Anonymous letter writing," he repeated thoughtfully. "What do you think that would accomplish?"

"Brings out people's true selves, don't you think? When you don't have to worry about what others expect, you can be exactly who you are." She paused, studying his face with the perceptiveness that came from decades of reading people. "Sometimes we need permission to be authentic. Sometimes anonymity gives us that permission."

After his grandmother returned to their house down the

street, Darius found himself thinking about her words. That evening, after locking up the store and climbing the narrow stairs to his apartment, he surveyed his small but comfortable space. One bedroom, a tiny kitchen, a living area with windows overlooking Main Street. Bookshelves lined every available wall, filled with classics, contemporary fiction, local histories, and notebooks containing his own attempts at capturing the stories he encountered daily.

It was his first real home away from his parents, his first space that belonged entirely to him. He'd arranged it carefully— a writing desk by the window where morning light would inspire productivity, comfortable reading chairs positioned to catch the afternoon sun, a small kitchen table where he could eat simple meals while reviewing the day's thoughts.

But it could feel lonely too, especially in the evenings when the street grew quiet and he was left with only his thoughts and half-finished stories for company. He'd written extensively during college, surrounded by peers who shared his interests and professors who encouraged his explorations. Here, his writing felt more solitary, disconnected from any community of readers or fellow writers who might provide feedback, encouragement, or simply the reassurance that someone else cared about the stories he was trying to tell.

When was the last time he'd been exactly who he was? In college, maybe, during late-night discussions about literature and philosophy. Or in his writing, when words flowed onto the page without regard for audience or approval. But in daily life, he often felt like he was performing a role—the dutiful grandson, the responsible business owner, the polite young man who listened more than he spoke because he'd learned that his thoughts often struck others as too intense for casual conversation.

The idea of anonymous correspondence appealed to him more than he expected. No assumptions about his age or background, no expectations based on his family connections or role as the bookstore's caretaker. Just thoughts on paper, shared with someone who might understand the peculiar loneliness of being surrounded by people yet feeling fundamentally unseen.

By the time he walked the two blocks to the library that evening, he'd made up his mind.

The library sat at the corner of Main and Oak, its brick building with ivy-covered walls and tall windows that glowed warmly in the evening light. Built in the 1920s with Carnegie Foundation funding, it had served as the town's intellectual hub for nearly a century. Inside, the original hardwood floors and oak shelving created an atmosphere of scholarly comfort that reminded Darius why he'd always felt at home among books.

Mrs Williams was reshelfing returns with the help of a young man Darius recognized as her grandson Chris.

"Darius!" Mrs Williams looked up with genuine pleasure. "What brings you by this evening?"

"I heard about your pen-pal program. My grandmother mentioned it."

"Of course she did." Mrs Williams chuckled, setting aside her books. "That woman has been trying to expand your social circle since you moved back. Smart lady—she knows isolation isn't good for creative souls."

Chris approached with a clipboard and friendly smile. "It's been really popular. We've got people from teenagers to retirees signing up."

"The program is about fostering authentic communication— something deeper than social media allows."

She handed Darius the familiar clipboard with its interest survey. He scanned the questions: *What do you hope to find through this program? What would you like to share about yourself? Describe your ideal conversation.*

"How does the matching work exactly?"

"I read through all the forms, looking for compatible interests and communication styles. Then I pair people up and deliver the first letters. After that, participants exchange letters through the library to maintain anonymity until both parties choose to reveal themselves."

Darius considered this. The idea of writing to someone who might actually want to hear his thoughts—about books, about dreams, about the strange liminal space of being twenty-four and uncertain—felt like discovering water after wandering in a desert.

"What kind of pen name should I choose?"

"Something that represents who you are when you're being most authentic," Mrs Williams suggested. "The person you are in your own mind, when no one else is watching or judging."

When no one else was watching, he was someone who noticed the way afternoon light transformed ordinary objects into something beautiful. Someone who believed stories had the power to change lives, who found meaning in the smallest details, who still thought it was possible to build something lasting and worthwhile in a world that often felt disposable and disconnected.

He thought about the trees surrounding Sweetgum—the oaks and maples that changed with seasons but remained rooted, the pines that stayed green through winter storms, providing shelter and consistency when everything else seemed uncertain.

He wrote

Evergreen

in careful letters.

Under "What you hope to find," he wrote:

Someone who values deep conversation over small

talk, who sees beauty in everyday moments, who believes words can bridge any distance between souls.

Under "What you'd like to share," he added:

A love of literature and history, questions about what makes life meaningful, observations about the world that others might find too philosophical for casual conversation.

Handing the clipboard back, he felt a flutter of nervous anticipation mixed with hope he hadn't experienced in months.

"Evergreen," Mrs Williams read with approval. "I like that. Steady, enduring, always growing toward the light."

As Darius walked home through the quiet streets of Sweetgum, he found himself looking forward to something for the first time in weeks. Somewhere in town, another person was hoping for the same kind of connection he craved. Someone who might understand that loneliness wasn't about being alone —it was about being unseen, unheard, misunderstood.

Back in his apartment, he looked out at Main Street with new eyes. The bookstore below held stories from decades past. His small space above contained possibilities for the future. And somewhere between the two, in letters yet to be written, might lie the connection he'd been seeking all along.

Maybe authentic conversation was only a letter away.

CHAPTER THREE

anielle pushed through the glass doors of Sweetgum Bookstore, inhaling the familiar scent of aged paper and something that might have been vanilla candles burning somewhere in the back. She'd spent her lunch break thinking about the pen-pal program, alternating between excitement and second-guessing herself. What if "Evergreen" turned out to be boring? What if she was the boring one? What if her responses revealed just how ordinary her thoughts really were when stripped of professional jargon and social pleasantries?

The store occupied a narrow but deep space on Main Street, with exposed brick walls lined floor to ceiling with book-shelves. Natural light streamed through tall windows, creating reading nooks that invited browsing. It was the kind of inde-pendent bookstore that felt like a living room rather than a retail space—comfortable chairs scattered throughout, hand-written shelf tags, and the sense that someone who truly loved books had arranged everything with care.

The store was quieter than usual for a Thursday afternoon, with only soft jazz playing from hidden speakers and the gentle rustle of someone browsing in the back corner. Behind the counter stood a man she'd seen around town but never really talked to—tall and lean, with short-cropped dark hair and a neatly trimmed beard that framed strong features. He wore a button-down shirt with the sleeves rolled up, revealing muscular forearms that suggested he spent time outdoors when he wasn't surrounded by books. Mr Jones's grandson, she remembered. He'd moved back recently to help with the family business.

She'd heard bits and pieces about him from her sisters—how he'd graduated from U-G-A with a degree in history, had some kind of opportunity in Atlanta that he'd turned down to come home and run the bookstore. The choice had puzzled most people in town, who couldn't understand why someone with his education would choose small-town retail over city career prospects.

He looked up as she approached, offering a polite smile that didn't quite reach his dark eyes. There was something guarded about his expression, as if he was perpetually braced for disappointment or judgment.

"Can I help you find something?"

"I'm looking for the newest book club selection for my sister." Danielle pulled out her phone to check Chrysta's text. "Kiss Me at the Hayride of Destiny by Penelope Puddlewick. Do you have it?"

"Fiction section, third shelf from the top." He gestured toward the back of the store without moving from behind the counter. "Should be several copies."

She waited for him to offer to show her, or at least come out from behind his fortress of paperwork, but he'd already returned to whatever he was doing—something involving a ledger and a stack of invoices that seemed to require intense concentration. His dismissal felt oddly impersonal, not rude exactly, but lacking the warmth she'd come to expect from local business owners.

Friendly, she thought with mild sarcasm, making her way toward the fiction section.

The books were exactly where he'd said they'd be, shelved alphabetically in a system that was clearly maintained with obsessive care. As she reached for a copy, she noticed the window display he'd arranged nearby. "Classic Literature for the Modern Reader," the handwritten sign proclaimed, showcasing leather-bound editions of Dickens, Austen, and Tolstoy alongside newer covers of the same works.

The display was undeniably beautiful—elegant, scholarly, designed to appeal to serious readers who appreciated literary heritage. But something about it bothered her. The books seemed to glower from their prominent position, like intellectual gatekeepers challenging passersby to prove their worthiness.

She found herself thinking about her own relationship with these titles. She'd read most of them in college, had even enjoyed several, but they represented a specific kind of reading experience—challenging, important, sometimes rewarding but rarely fun. When she thought about books that had made her fall in love with reading, they weren't in this display. Where were the stories that made people stay up past midnight because they couldn't put them down?

She studied the display for another moment, then returned to the counter with both the book club selection and a slight frown.

"Interesting window display," she said as he rang up her purchase.

"Thank you." His tone suggested the conversation was over, but there was a hint of pride in his posture that told her the display was his own creation.

"Though I have to ask—do you really think everyone walking by wants to be intimidated by War and Peace before they've even entered the store?"

Now she had his attention. He looked up, dark eyes focusing on her with new interest and what might have been defensiveness. "Intimidated?"

"Come on." Danielle gestured toward the window, warming to her argument. "You've basically created a literary gatekeeping situation. 'Welcome to our bookstore. Hope you're smart enough to shop here.'"

His face darkened, and she could see him straightening slightly, preparing to defend his choices. "I prefer to think of it as encouraging people to challenge themselves. There's nothing wrong with aspiring to read something substantial."

The word "substantial" carried an implication that made her bristle—as if books that weren't centuries-old classics were somehow insubstantial, lightweight, unworthy of serious consideration.

"And there's nothing wrong with reading for pleasure either. Where are the books that make people excited to come inside? The ones that promise escape and adventure instead of home-work assignments?"

"Those are throughout the store." His voice had taken on a lecture-like quality that probably served him well in academic discussions but felt condescending in casual conversation. "The window display is meant to highlight—"

"Your intellectual superiority?" The words came out sharper than she'd intended, but something about his defensive posture irritated her. She'd encountered this attitude before—the assumption that literary merit was inversely proportional to accessibility, that truly smart people naturally gravitated toward difficult texts.

His jaw tightened, and she could see she'd struck a nerve. "My respect for literature that has endured for good reason. Not everything needs to be dumbed down for mass consumption."

"Wow." Danielle blinked at him, genuinely taken aback by the implication. "Did you just suggest that people who don't read Tolstoy are consuming dumbed-down literature?"

"That's not what I—" He stopped, running a hand over his short hair in what seemed to be a nervous gesture. She could see him realizing how his words had sounded, could watch him trying to figure out how to backtrack without losing his argument entirely. "Look, I'm trying to elevate the conversation around books, not exclude people."

"By putting the most intimidating titles you could find in the window? By suggesting that popular books are somehow lesser?"

"By showcasing works that have shaped human thought for centuries." His passion was evident now, not just defensiveness but genuine belief in what he was saying. "These books have endured because they offer something that transcendent literature provides—insight into the human condition, artistic merit that stands the test of time."

Danielle felt a reluctant spark of admiration for his conviction, even as his intellectual snobbery continued to annoy her. There was something compelling about someone who cared so deeply about books, even if his approach felt misguided. She tucked a curl behind her ear, leaning forward slightly.

"Okay, but counter-argument: maybe save the literary education for people who are already inside and browsing. Use the window to invite people in, not to prove how well-read you are."

They stared at each other across the counter, the air crackling with tension that felt oddly electric. Up close, she could see the way he pressed his lips together when thinking, could notice how his dark eyes seemed to see straight through her careful defenses. There was intelligence there, intensity, but also something that looked like loneliness—as if he was used to having these conversations with himself rather than with people who might push back.

The silence stretched for several heartbeats, and she became aware of how quiet the store had grown around them. Even the jazz music seemed to have faded into background whisper.

"What would you put in the window?" he asked finally, his voice carrying a challenge but also what sounded like genuine curiosity.

The question energized her, made her realize she'd been thinking about this exact issue since she'd first seen his display. "Books that make people dream. Romance novels with gorgeous covers that promise emotional journeys. Thrillers that make you want to clear your evening schedule because you know you won't be able to put them down. Fantasy series that transport you to worlds where magic is possible and heroes always find a way to save the day."

She leaned against the counter, warming to her theme and unconsciously commanding the space between them. Her enthusiasm was building as she spoke, fueled by memories of books that had shaped her own love of reading.

"Memoirs that make you laugh until you snort coffee and cry until you need tissues. Young adult novels that remind adults what it felt like to believe the whole world was ahead of them. Stories that remind people why they fell in love with reading in the first place, before teachers made them analyze the symbolism in everything and write essays about themes instead of just enjoying the ride."

His expression had shifted as she spoke, the defensiveness giving way to something more complex—part frustration, part curiosity, part what looked like reluctant respect for her passion.

"And you don't think people can fall in love with Austen? With Dickens?"

"Of course they can. But maybe start with Pride and Prejudice and Zombies before you throw Mansfield Park at them. Maybe acknowledge that reading Outlander might lead someone to historical fiction in general, which might eventually lead them to Jane Eyre. Meet people where they are instead of demanding they climb up to where you think they should be."

He studied her with an expression she found hard to read—part frustration, part curiosity, and something that might have been admiration for her willingness to challenge him so directly.

"You seem to have strong opinions about bookstore marketing for someone who..." He trailed off, clearly thinking better of whatever he'd been about to say.

"For someone who what? Doesn't look like I read the classics?" Heat flashed through her, her pulse quickening. She could feel her cheeks warming with indignation. "For someone who works with numbers instead of novels?"

"That's not what I meant."

"Then what did you mean?" She leaned forward slightly, close enough to catch the scent of his cologne—something clean and masculine that made her unexpectedly aware of him as more than just an opponent in a literary debate.

He was quiet for a moment, clearly struggling with something. She could see him weighing his words, trying to figure out how to express whatever he was thinking without making things worse.

Finally, he said, "For someone who doesn't seem to understand that some things are worth preserving, even if they're not immediately accessible. That maybe the challenge of great literature is part of what makes it valuable."

"And you don't seem to understand that turning people away at the door doesn't preserve anything—it just makes you feel superior while your customer base shrinks and independent bookstores close because they can't compete with online retailers who don't judge their customers' reading choices."

The silence stretched between them again, charged with an energy that made Danielle's heart race. She should probably apologize for being so confrontational, should take her book and leave before she said something she'd regret. Instead, she found herself studying the way his shoulders had tensed, the slight clenching of his jaw when he was passionate about something.

There was something attractive about his intensity, even when it was directed toward defending positions she disagreed with. She could see why he'd chosen to come back and run this store rather than pursue some corporate career—he genuinely cared about books, about literature, about the role stories played in people's lives. His approach might be misguided, but his passion was real.

"Your total is $14.99," he said finally, his voice carefully neutral.

She handed over her credit card, hyperaware of the brush of their fingers when he returned it. His hands were warm, steady, with calluses that suggested he did more than just handle books and paperwork.

"Thanks."

"Will there be anything else?"

The question was clearly meant to dismiss her, but something rebellious in Danielle's chest made her linger. Maybe it was the way he'd actually listened to her arguments instead of just dismissing her. Maybe it was curiosity about whether he'd consider what she'd said or simply write her off as someone who didn't understand serious literature.

"Actually, yes. I'm curious to see if you'll take the challenge."

"What challenge?"

"Change your window display. Try something that invites people in instead of testing their literary credentials. See if it makes a difference in foot traffic, in sales, in the kinds of conversations you have with customers."

He raised an eyebrow, and she could see him considering the proposition despite himself. "And if it doesn't work?"

"Then I'll come back and publicly admit that Sweetgum is full of people who prefer intimidating classics to accessible stories. I'll even help you rearrange your display to be even more impressively scholarly."

"And if it does work?"

Danielle grinned, feeling more alive than she had all day. The conversation had energized her in a way that reminded her why she'd once loved debating literature in college seminars. "Then you admit that meeting people where they are is better than making them climb up to where you think they should be. And maybe you consider that accessibility and literary merit aren't mutually exclusive."

She left the store before he could respond, but not before she caught the slight smile tugging at the corner of his mouth—as if despite himself, he was intrigued by her challenge.

Outside, her heart was racing in a way that had nothing to do with the September heat. The afternoon sun felt warm on her face as she walked back toward her office, and she found herself replaying the conversation, analyzing the way his expression had shifted as they'd talked.

Well, that had been unexpected. She'd gone in for a simple book purchase and ended up in a full-scale literary debate with someone who clearly took his books very seriously. Too seriously, maybe, but she had to admit there was something appealing about his passion, even when it was misdirected.

The way he'd defended his position showed real conviction, not just intellectual posturing. And the moment when he'd asked what she would put in the window—that had felt like genuine curiosity, not just rhetorical challenge. Maybe underneath all that literary snobbery was someone who actually wanted to connect with readers, who just didn't know how to bridge the gap between his academic background and the practical realities of running a small business.

As she walked back to work, Danielle found herself

wondering if he'd actually take her challenge. Probably not—he seemed like the type who'd rather be right than admit when someone else had a point. But there had been something in his expression at the end, a flicker of interest that suggested he might at least consider what she'd said.

Still, she made a mental note to walk past the bookstore tomorrow on her lunch break. Purely to see if her argument had made any impact on that intimidating window display, of course.

The fact that she was curious about the man behind the counter—about what had driven him to choose this life, about whether his intensity extended beyond literary debates, about what it might be like to have a conversation with him when they weren't arguing—was completely irrelevant.

Or so she told herself as she climbed the stairs to her office, still feeling energized by an encounter that had reminded her how much she'd missed having her ideas taken seriously by someone who wasn't afraid to push back.

CHAPTER FOUR

*D*arius stared at the window display he'd so carefully arranged that morning, then at the book still sitting on the counter where the challenging woman had left her credit card receipt. Danielle something—he'd glimpsed her name when she'd signed, though he'd been too flustered by their verbal sparring match to catch her last name.

He ran a hand over his close-cropped hair, still feeling the electric tension that had crackled between them. In the three months he'd been running the bookstore, most customer interactions followed predictable patterns: polite inquiries, gentle suggestions, pleasant but forgettable exchanges. Mrs Patterson with her weekly romance novels, Mr Chen looking for gardening books, teenagers browsing the graphic novel section while trying to look sophisticated. No one had ever challenged his curatorial choices with such passionate conviction.

Or looked at him with those dark eyes that seemed to see straight through his carefully constructed intellectual defenses.

The afternoon light had shifted since their confrontation, casting different shadows across his display. From this angle, the leather-bound classics did look somewhat forbidding—

stately and impressive, yes, but hardly welcoming. He found himself seeing them through her eyes: War and Peace glowering from its prominent position like a literary bouncer, Moby Dick seeming to dare browsers to attempt its waters, the collected works of Shakespeare arranged like an entrance exam to some exclusive literary club.

Had he really created a barrier instead of an invitation? The thought unsettled him more than he wanted to admit.

The bell above the door chimed, and his grandmother entered with a knowing smile and a covered plate.

"Thought you might want some dinner," she said, setting the plate on the counter with the care of someone who'd been feeding family for decades. "Leftovers from Sunday's pot roast."

"Thanks, Grandma." He lifted the foil, breathing in the familiar scents of home cooking that always reminded him why he'd chosen to come back to Sweetgum. "How was your book club?"

"Enlightening. We discussed marketing strategies for local businesses." Her eyes twinkled with mischief as she glanced toward his window display. "Someone mentioned that your classics showcase might be a bit... intimidating for casual browsers."

Darius felt heat rise in his neck. The timing was too perfect to be coincidental. "Let me guess—Mrs Andrews from the hit-and-run squad?"

"Actually, it was that lovely Danielle Jacobs. She stopped by the library after leaving here, mentioned your conversation about accessible versus aspirational literature." His grandmother's smile widened with the particular satisfaction of someone whose matchmaking instincts had been activated. "Quite the passionate young woman, from what I heard."

"She certainly has opinions." He tried to keep his voice neutral, but something in his tone must have given him away because his grandmother's eyebrows rose with interest.

"The kind of opinions that make a person think, I'd imagine. Those can be valuable, especially for someone who spends too much time alone with his books."

Before he could respond, she was already heading toward the door with the efficient movement of someone who'd said exactly what she'd come to say. "Don't stay up too late, dear. And maybe consider whether that window display truly represents what you want to say to the community."

Alone again, Darius found himself studying his arrangement with new eyes. The leather-bound classics did look formidable, he had to admit. When he'd created the display, he'd been thinking about permanence, about the enduring value of literature that had survived centuries of changing tastes. He'd wanted to honor the tradition of serious reading, to suggest that this bookstore was a place where important conversations about significant works could happen.

But looking at it now, he could see how it might appear to someone like Danielle—like a test rather than an invitation, a challenge rather than a welcome. How many potential customers had walked past, assuming they weren't smart enough or serious enough to belong in a store that showcased such intimidating fare?

The woman was infuriating. She'd walked into his store and immediately criticized his choices, questioned his approach, and made him defend positions he'd never actually examined critically. She'd been blunt to the point of rudeness, challenging his expertise in his own domain without any apparent awareness of his background or credentials.

But she'd also been alive in a way that most people in Sweetgum weren't. Sharp, funny, unafraid to challenge him when she thought he was wrong. There had been genuine passion in her arguments, not just contrarian spirit but real conviction about the importance of making literature accessible to people who might otherwise feel excluded.

And the way she'd leaned against the counter while making her case, her curls catching the afternoon light, her eyes flashing with conviction—he'd found it harder to concentrate on their debate than he cared to admit. When was the last time someone had engaged with him so directly, so fearlessly?

His phone buzzed with a text from Chris at the library.

Got your first pen-pal letter! Come by whenever
to pick it up.

Darius's pulse quickened. In the aftermath of his encounter with Danielle, he'd nearly forgotten about the letter program. Now the prospect of connecting with "Maplewood Muse" offered a welcome distraction from replaying every moment of his argument with the challenging woman from the bookstore.

He locked up early, something he'd never done before, and walked the two blocks to the library through the gathering dusk. The evening air carried the scent of wood-smoke and the last roses of summer, and Main Street looked different somehow—less like a stage where he performed the role of responsible business owner and more like a community where real conversations might be possible.

Mrs Williams handed him the envelope with obvious delight, as if she were facilitating something magical rather than simply passing along mail. "I have such a good feeling about this match," she said with the satisfaction of someone whose instincts had proven reliable over decades of bringing people together.

Twenty minutes later, he was back in his apartment above the store, settled into his favorite armchair by the window over-looking Main Street. The envelope felt substantial in his hands, and he found himself hesitating before opening it, savoring the anticipation of discovering who Maplewood Muse might be.

The letter was written in flowing handwriting on cream-colored paper that suggested someone who took the physical act of letter writing seriously. He unfolded it carefully and began to read.

Dear Evergreen,

Mrs Williams matched us based on our interest in meaningful conversation and authentic connection, so I hope you won't mind if I dive right into the deep end. I've been thinking about your question regarding what makes life meaningful, and I keep coming back to the idea that we find meaning in the stories we tell ourselves about our experiences.

For instance, I spend my days analyzing data, finding patterns in numbers that help businesses make decisions. It's practical work, necessary work, but it doesn't feed my soul. What feeds my soul is the story I tell myself about those numbers—that behind each data point is a person making choices, following dreams, building a life. The spreadsheets become secondary to the human narratives they represent.

I'm curious about your work with literature and history. Do you find that old stories still speak to modern hearts? Sometimes I worry that we've become so focused on immediate gratification that we've lost the patience for stories that unfold slowly, that require us to sit with uncertainty and complex emotions.

What draws you to the past? What do you hope to find there that the present can't provide?

Looking forward to your thoughts,
Maplewood Muse.

P.S. I had the most interesting debate today with someone about the accessibility of literature. Made me realize how passionate I can become about ensuring stories reach the people who need them most. Do you ever find yourself defending books to people who think they're not "smart enough" for certain authors?

Darius set the letter down with hands that trembled slightly. The coincidence was too striking to ignore—Maplewood Muse had had a debate about literature accessibility on the same day he'd argued with Danielle about his window display. But surely it was just that, a coincidence. Sweetgum was small enough that literary discussions were probably rare enough to make any such conversation notable to someone who craved intellectual engagement.

He read the letter again, captivated by her voice on the page. She wrote the way he'd always imagined his ideal conversation partner would think—thoughtfully, with depth and nuance, unafraid of complex ideas but grounded in practical experience. Her perspective on finding meaning in everyday work resonated deeply; he'd been struggling with similar questions about the value of preserving literary culture in a world that seemed increasingly uninterested in anything that couldn't be consumed quickly.

There was something about her voice that felt familiar.

Maybe it was simply the recognition of a kindred spirit—someone else who believed that stories mattered, that literature had the power to illuminate human experience in ways that nothing else could.

Moving to his small desk by the window, he pulled out paper and pen, composing his response with more care than he'd given to anything in months. The words seemed to flow from somewhere deeper than his usual analytical mind, as if Maplewood Muse's openness was giving him permission to be equally honest.

Dear Maplewood Muse,

Your letter arrived at the perfect moment—I've been questioning whether old stories truly matter in our fast-paced world, and your perspective on finding human narratives within data points offers a beautiful answer. Yes, I believe classic literature still speaks to modern hearts, but perhaps we need better translators, people who can help others see past the intimidating reputation these works have acquired.

You ask what draws me to the past. I think I'm searching for proof that human nature hasn't fundamentally changed, that the struggles and triumphs of people centuries ago can illuminate our own experiences. When I read Austen's sharp observations about social dynamics or Dickens's compassion for the marginalized, I feel connected to something larger than my own small corner of existence.

But I'll confess something: today someone challenged me on exactly the point you raised in your postscript. They accused me of creating barriers instead of bridges, of prioritizing my own intellectual pride over genuine accessibility. The criticism stung because I recognized its truth—I have been defensive about literature, as if protecting it from dilution was more important than sharing it generously.

Your correspondent sounds like someone worth listening to. Perhaps they understand something about reaching hearts that I'm still learning.

What stories have shaped you? I'd love to know what books made you fall in love with reading, before literature became something to debate rather than simply experience.

Eagerly awaiting your reply,
Evergreen

As he sealed the envelope, Darius found himself wondering about the mysterious Maplewood Muse. Her intelligence and warmth were evident in every line, and her perspective challenged him in ways that felt productive rather than threatening. She seemed like someone who would understand his love of books while also pushing him to examine his assumptions about how to share that love with others.

Unlike a certain sharp-tongued bookstore customer who'd spent their entire conversation making him feel defensive about his choices. Though, he had to admit, both women had succeeded in making him question his approach to sharing literature with others. Maybe that was exactly what he needed— people who cared enough to challenge him when he was wrong, who pushed him to be better rather than simply validating his existing beliefs.

The parallel between his two encounters that day wasn't lost on him. Both Danielle and Maplewood Muse seemed to believe that literature should be accessible, that stories belonged to everyone rather than just to people with the right education or background. Both had challenged him to think beyond his own perspective, to consider how his choices might affect others.

Walking to the window, he looked down at his display with new understanding. Tomorrow, he'd take Danielle's dare and create something more inviting. Not because she'd demanded it, but because both she and Maplewood Muse had helped him realize that his love of books meant nothing if he kept them locked away from the people who might need them most.

The thought of seeing Danielle's surprise when she discovered his change of heart sent an unexpected thrill through him. He told himself it was simple intellectual curiosity—he wanted to see if she'd acknowledge when someone took her advice. He was curious whether she'd be gracious in victory or whether she'd find new aspects of his approach to criticize.

It had nothing to do with the way her eyes had lit up during their argument, or how her passion had made him feel more awake than he had in a while. Nothing to do with the way she'd challenged him so fearlessly, or how she'd made him want to be worthy of that challenge.

Nothing at all.

But as he prepared for bed, Darius found himself looking forward to tomorrow in a way he hadn't experienced since moving back to Sweetgum. Two women had entered his life in a single day—one through anonymous correspondence, one through direct confrontation—and both had reminded him that books were meant to be shared, discussed, celebrated rather than hoarded like intellectual treasures.

Maybe tomorrow would bring more surprises, more challenges to his assumptions, more reminders that the world was full of people worth getting to know.

Maybe tomorrow would be the beginning of exactly the kind of authentic connection he'd been seeking all along.

CHAPTER FIVE

*D*anielle sat in her car outside Roasted Beans Coffee Spot, phone pressed to her ear as she watched the morning rush through the café windows. The familiar red and white storefront had been part of her daily routine for two years, but today everything felt different somehow—charged with possibility in a way that made even mundane Tuesday morning rituals seem significant.

She'd gotten Aleeyah's voicemail at seven AM and called back immediately, needing her sister's voice to ground her after a restless night of thinking about bookstore owners and anonymous pen pals. Sleep had been elusive, her mind cycling between anticipation about receiving her first letter from "Evergreen" and replaying every moment of her heated debate with the infuriatingly attractive man behind the bookstore counter.

"Finally!" Aleeyah's voice came through warm and slightly breathless. "I was starting to think you were avoiding me."

"Never. Just busy with work stuff." Danielle shifted in her seat, watching a familiar figure walk past—Mrs Andrews from the hit-and-run squad, power-walking in a bright pink tracksuit that could probably be seen from space. The woman moved with the determined efficiency of someone who'd appointed herself unofficial monitor of downtown Sweetgum's morning activities.

"What's up?"

"I wanted to hear about this pen-pal thing. Chrysta mentioned you signed up for some letter-writing program?" There was that particular tone Aleeyah used when she was trying to sound casual about something that had clearly been the subject of family discussion.

Leave it to Chrysta to spread family news before Danielle was ready to discuss it. Her sisters meant well, but sometimes their protective instincts felt more like surveillance. "It's nothing dramatic. Just an anonymous correspondence thing the library started. Thought it might be fun."

"Anonymous, huh?" Aleeyah's tone carried that particular mix of amusement and concern that came with being the middle sister who'd watched both her siblings navigate various romantic disasters. "Please tell me you're not planning to fall in love with some stranger through the mail."

"It's not about romance," Danielle protested, though she felt heat creep up her neck at the suggestion. Was that what people would think? That she was so desperate for connection she'd resorted to Victorian-era courtship methods? "It's about mean-ingful conversation. Finding someone who wants to talk about more than the weather and what happened on last night's TV show."

The truth was more complicated, though. She'd signed up hoping for intellectual stimulation, but she couldn't deny the flutter of romantic possibility that had accompanied her deci-sion. In a town the size of Sweetgum, eligible bachelors weren't exactly abundant, and the anonymity of letter writing elimi-nated the awkwardness of first dates and the pressure of imme-diate physical chemistry.

"Mmm-hmm. And how's that going?"

Danielle thought about the anticipation she'd felt signing up, the nervous excitement of wondering what kind of person "Evergreen" might be. The name suggested someone stable, enduring, perhaps with a love of nature or literature. Someone who'd chosen a pseudonym that spoke to permanence rather than flash.

"I don't know yet. Mrs Williams is still doing the matching process." She paused, watching a young mother push a stroller past the café while juggling a coffee cup and phone. "She said she'd have first letters ready by today or tomorrow."

"Well, just promise me you'll be careful. I know you're feeling left out with Chrysta and me both settled, but—"

"This isn't about feeling left out," Danielle interrupted, though she knew it partly was. Watching both her sisters find love had been wonderful and isolating in equal measure. Chrysta's whirlwind romance with Terrence, Aleeyah's fairy-tale wedding to Greg—both had found their people, their places, their happily-ever-afters. Meanwhile, Danielle felt like she was still waiting for her story to begin.

"It's about wanting real connection," she continued. "When's the last time someone asked me what I actually think about something important? What I dream about beyond quarterly reports and weekend plans?"

Aleeyah was quiet for a moment, and Danielle could picture her sister's expression—the slight furrow between her brows that appeared whenever she was processing something serious. "That bad at work, huh?"

"It's not the work itself. It's just..." Danielle struggled to find words for the restlessness that had been building for months like pressure in a kettle. "I feel like I'm disappearing into spreadsheets and data points. Like the most interesting thing about me is how quickly I can analyze a profit-loss statement."

She watched a group of teenagers walk past, laughing and animated, probably discussing some drama that felt earth-shattering in the way that only high school problems could. When had she stopped feeling that passionate about anything? When had her conversations become so safe, so predictable, so utterly forgettable?

"You know that's not true."

"Do I? Because yesterday I got into this ridiculous argument with some guy at the bookstore about literature accessibility, and it was the most alive I've felt in weeks. How pathetic is that?"

The admission surprised her with its honesty. She hadn't meant to reveal quite so much about her current emotional state, but something about Aleeyah's voice made it easy to be more transparent than usual.

"What kind of argument?" Aleeyah's voice perked up with interest, and Danielle could hear the shift from concerned sister to invested audience.

Danielle found herself describing her encounter with the bookstore owner's grandson—his pretentious window display, their heated exchange about meeting readers where they are versus challenging them to reach higher. As she talked, she could picture him clearly: the way his jaw had tightened when she'd challenged his choices, how his dark eyes had focused on her with such intensity, the passionate conviction in his voice when he'd defended his literary philosophy.

She described the elegant but intimidating arrangement of classics, her criticism of his gatekeeping approach, his defensive response about elevating literary conversation. The more she talked, the more she realized how much the encounter had affected her—not just intellectually, but physically. Her pulse had raced during their debate in a way that had nothing to do with anger and everything to do with the thrill of being truly engaged with another person.

"He was so convinced that he was doing something noble," she explained, stopping at a red light and catching her reflection in the rearview mirror. "Like he was preserving culture single-handedly through window displays. But he couldn't see that intimidating people isn't the same as inspiring them."

"So let me get this straight," Aleeyah said when she finished. "You walked into a bookstore, picked a fight with a complete stranger about his marketing strategy, and came away feeling more energized than you have in months?"

"I didn't pick a fight. I made an observation." But even as she said it, Danielle knew Aleeyah was right. She had deliberately provoked the conversation, had pushed harder than necessary when a polite suggestion might have sufficed.

"Danielle." Aleeyah's laugh was warm and knowing, with the particular affection that came from years of sisterly observation. "You absolutely picked a fight. The question is why."

"Because his display was elitist and exclusionary." The defense came automatically, but she could hear how hollow it sounded even to her own ears.

"Uh-huh. And what did this literary gatekeeper look like?"

"That's not—why does that matter?" But even as Danielle protested, she could feel her pulse quicken at the memory of his strong features, the way his rolled sleeves had revealed muscular forearms as he'd gestured during their debate. The neat beard that framed his mouth, the way his eyes had darkened when he was passionate about something.

"Oh my God, he was attractive." Aleeyah sounded delighted, and Danielle could practically hear her sister's grin through the phone. "You picked a fight with a hot guy who takes books seriously. No wonder you felt alive."

"I did not—" Danielle stopped, recognizing the futility of denial when Aleeyah was in detective mode. Her sister had always been too perceptive for comfortable family conversations. "Okay, fine. He was attractive. But he was also insufferably pretentious."

"The best ones usually are. Means they care about something

passionately, even if they're wrong about how to express it." Aleeyah paused, and Danielle could hear what sounded like coffee brewing in the background. "Did you get his name?"

"I wasn't trying to get his name. I was making a point about customer accessibility." Though she had noticed his name on the credit card receipt she'd signed—something Jones, like his grandfather. She'd been too flustered by their verbal sparring to catch his first name.

"Right. And are you planning to go back and see if he took your challenge?"

Danielle had been planning exactly that, though she'd been trying not to admit it to herself. The prospect of seeing whether he'd actually changed his display had been occupying her thoughts since she'd woken up. Would he prove himself as stubborn as she'd assumed, or would he surprise her by showing some flexibility?

"Maybe. For research purposes."

"Research." Aleeyah's tone was dry with amusement. "Well, just promise me you won't get so caught up in sparring with Mr Bookstore that you forget to give your pen pal a fair chance. Anonymous letters might lead somewhere interesting too."

"I know." And she did know, intellectually. The pen-pal program represented exactly the kind of meaningful connection she'd been craving—someone who wanted to explore ideas, share thoughts, engage with life on a deeper level than surface pleasantries. But the thought of her mysterious correspondent didn't make her pulse race the way the memory of yesterday's argument did.

"I should probably get to work," she said, checking the time on her dashboard.

"Call me after you get your first letter, okay? I want to hear all about this Evergreen person. And maybe about any follow-up visits to certain bookstores."

"Aleeyah—"

"I'm just saying, when's the last time someone made you feel alive? Even if it was through arguing?" Her sister's voice carried the wisdom of someone who'd found her own unexpected love story. "Don't dismiss that feeling just because it came wrapped in literary snobbery."

After hanging up, Danielle sat in her car for another moment, watching the morning foot traffic on Main Street. The sidewalks were busy with the usual Tuesday rhythm—commuters heading to work, shop owners setting up for the day, elderly residents beginning their morning constitutional walks. It was a scene she'd observed hundreds of times, but today it felt different somehow, full of possibility rather than routine.

She could see the bookstore from here, its windows catching the early light. The brick facade looked warm and inviting in the morning sun, with hanging planters that suggested someone cared about creating a welcoming atmosphere. Had he changed his display? Was he even thinking about their conversation, or had she been just another difficult customer in his day?

The smart thing would be to focus on the pen-pal program, to give "Evergreen" her full attention when his letter arrived. Anonymous correspondence was safe, intellectual, free from the complications of physical attraction and personality clashes. She could explore ideas without worrying about how she looked or whether her arguments came across as too aggressive or whether the other person was judging her based on assumptions about her appearance or background.

But as she finally headed into Roasted Beans for her morning coffee, Danielle found herself hoping that whoever Evergreen turned out to be, he'd have at least half the passion she'd seen in those dark eyes yesterday. Even if that passion had been directed at defending literary snobbery.

The coffee shop was busier than usual, with a line that gave her time to think. Maybe Aleeyah was right—maybe she shouldn't dismiss the feeling of being truly engaged, even if it had come through conflict. How long had it been since someone had challenged her intellectually? Since she'd felt moved to defend her own beliefs with such conviction?

Her job required analytical thinking, but it rarely demanded creativity or passion. Her social life in Sweetgum was pleasant but rarely profound. Yesterday's argument had reminded her that she had opinions, strong ones, and that expressing them didn't make her difficult—it made her interesting.

Because Aleeyah was right about one thing—she had felt more alive during that ten-minute argument than she had in months. And now she wanted more of that feeling, whether it came through anonymous letters or face-to-face debates with infuriatingly articulate men who cared too much about classic literature.

The anticipation of both possibilities carried her through the morning, making even her spreadsheet analysis feel lighter. She found herself approaching her data with more curiosity than usual, looking for the human stories behind the numbers in a way that reminded her of how she'd described her work in the pen-pal application.

For the first time in forever, she was looking forward to her lunch break—and the walk past a certain bookstore window that would tell her whether yesterday's argument had made any impact at all. Whether the man behind the counter was as stubborn as she'd assumed, or whether he might surprise her by proving he could listen as passionately as he could argue.

Either way, she was about to find out.

CHAPTER SIX

*D*arius stood before his transformed window display on Thursday morning, watching steam rise from his coffee mug in the cool September air. Two days had passed since he'd completely overhauled his arrangement, and the familiar weight of doubt had settled into a persistent hum of uncertainty.

Gone were the intimidating classics he'd removed Tuesday evening after his confrontation with Danielle. In their place: a riot of color and promise that would have scandalized his literature professors. *My Heart Belongs to a Vampire Accountant* by Moonbeam Fluffernutter commanded center stage, its glittery cover practically vibrating with supernatural romance. He'd surrounded it with books that had surprised him with their emotional punch—*The Duchess and the Dragon Dentist* promising historical hijinks, *Love in the Time of Pickle Factories* with its quirky small-town charm, and yes, *Kissed by a Cowboy Named Kevin* which had made him laugh out loud in ways that Dickens never had.

His new sign read simply: "Books That Keep You Up Past Midnight."

The honesty of it still terrified him after forty-eight hours. These weren't books that would impress visiting professors or demonstrate his intellectual credentials. They were books that had made him forget to eat dinner, that had him reading by phone flashlight under covers like a teenager hiding contraband.

Yesterday had brought a steady stream of curious browsers —more foot traffic than he'd seen in weeks. Mrs Henderson had actually purchased *Zombies in My Wedding Dress*, her first novel in twenty years. Three teenagers had spent an hour debating the merits of various fantasy series. Even Mr Chen had paused to flip through *The Great Turnip Heist*, chuckling at the back cover copy.

But he hadn't seen Danielle since that first morning when she'd walked past, done a double-take, and taken a photo of his window with what looked like approval.

The bell announced his grandmother's arrival, along with the scent of fresh coffee cake that meant she was pleased about something.

"How's the great literary experiment progressing?" she asked, noting the small stack of sales receipts from yesterday.

"Better than expected. Though I keep waiting for someone to tell me I've destroyed the intellectual integrity of the store."

She studied his arrangement with the shrewd eye of someone who'd watched him grow from a boy who hid *Captain Underpants* behind textbooks to a man still doing essentially the same thing.

"Sometimes destruction is just another word for making room for growth." She patted his shoulder. "Your great-aunt would have approved. She always said books were meant to find their readers, not intimidate them."

At ten-fifteen, Chris Williams bounded through the door with the energy of someone caffeinated beyond reason.

"Special delivery from headquarters," he announced,

producing an envelope with a flourish. "My grandmother is practically giddy about how well the letter exchanges are going. People are already asking about second rounds of correspondence."

Darius accepted the letter with hands steadier than he felt. The envelope was addressed in the same careful script as before, but something about it seemed different—more confident, perhaps, or simply more familiar.

Dear Evergreen,

I've been thinking about margins—not the kind in my spreadsheets, but the spaces where readers write their truest thoughts. You mentioned feeling defensive about literature, and it made me wonder: what if our defensiveness comes from loving something so much we're afraid of sharing it wrong?

I had coffee yesterday with someone who collects vintage books, and she told me something interesting. She said the most valuable books in her collection aren't the pristine first editions—they're the ones previous owners loved enough to damage. Dog-eared pages, broken spines, coffee stains that tell stories about late-night reading sessions.

Maybe that's what authentic literary culture looks like: not preservation, but transformation. Books that change because they've changed people.

Speaking of change, I walked past a bookstore two days ago where someone had completely redesigned their window display. Instead of intimidating classics, they'd chosen books that looked like adventures waiting to happen. It made me want to go inside and discover something new, which I think might be exactly the point.

Do you think it's possible to love something deeply while holding it lightly? To care passionately without becoming possessive?

Yours in curiosity,
Maplewood Muse

P.S. I started re-reading Passion at Pemberly Manor last night and found myself writing in the margins for the first time in years. "Darcy, you magnificent mess," being just one example. Somehow it felt like coming home.

Darius read the letter three times, each pass revealing new layers. The timing felt deliberate—her mention of walking past a bookstore two days ago, her observations about transformation and authenticity. But more than coincidence, he sensed a kindred spirit wrestling with the same questions about passion and possessiveness that had kept him awake since his confrontation with Danielle.

Her image of valuable books being the damaged ones struck him particularly. He thought of his own library upstairs—the pristine copies he'd never dared mark up, and the battered paperbacks he returned to when he needed comfort rather than education.

He pulled out fresh paper, surprising himself by reaching for his fountain pen instead of the ballpoint he usually used for correspondence.

Dear Maplewood Muse,

Your question about loving deeply while holding lightly might be the most important thing anyone's asked me in years. I think I've been confusing protection with possession, treating literature like a finite resource that diminishes when shared rather than a living thing that grows stronger through connection.

That bookstore you mentioned—I suspect I know which one. The owner recently had his assumptions challenged by someone who wasn't afraid to tell him his approach was failing. Initially defensive, he's discovering that being wrong about methods doesn't invalidate caring about outcomes.

You're right about damaged books holding more value. I have a copy of Pirates, Parrots, and Passionate Encounters that's literally falling apart because I've read it so many times. Every torn page represents a moment of joy, every stain a memory of being so absorbed I forgot the world existed. Meanwhile, my pristine hardcover edition of Melancholy Musings on Mortality sits untouched on the shelf, beautiful and essentially meaningless.

I'm learning that maybe the goal isn't to create perfect readers, but to create passionate ones. People who write "Darcy, you magnificent mess" in margins are exactly the kind of readers literature needs.

Thank you for helping me see the difference between gatekeeping and shepherding. One keeps people out; the other guides them home.

Gratefully yours,

Evergreen

P.S. If you're reading Passion at Pemberly Manor with fresh eyes, you might enjoy knowing that the author was told her novel was "coarse" and "disagreeable" by critics who preferred more refined literature. Sometimes the books that change us are the ones that refuse to behave properly.

As he sealed the envelope, movement outside caught his attention. Danielle Jacobs was walking past again, this time slowing deliberately to study his window display. She pulled out her phone and appeared to be looking at something on the screen, then glanced back at his window with what looked like a satisfied expression.

This time, she pushed through his door.

"So," she said, approaching the counter with a slight smile, "I have to know. Did you actually take the challenge, or is this just coincidental redecorating?"

The directness of her question sent heat up his neck, but also something that felt suspiciously like delight. "What do you think?"

"I think," she said, studying his face with those disconcerting dark eyes, "that you're either very adaptable or very stubborn, and I'm trying to figure out which."

"Can't I be both?"

Her laugh was warm and genuine. "That might be the most honest thing you've said since I met you."

For the first time since returning to Sweetgum, he felt like he was exactly where he was supposed to be.

CHAPTER SEVEN

The following day, Danielle stepped into Rochelle's Old-Fashioned Diner just as the lunch rush was hitting full swing, the familiar brass bell above the door announcing her arrival with its cheerful chime. The familiar sounds of clinking silverware and cheerful conversation washed over her, along with the mouthwatering aroma of fried chicken and fresh biscuits that had been drawing locals to this corner establishment for many years.

She'd been riding a wave of satisfaction since her visit to the bookstore yesterday, when she'd discovered that Darius had not only taken her challenge but had transformed his entire window into something that made her want to applaud. *My Heart Belongs to a Vampire Accountant* by Moonbeam Fluffernutter prominently displayed alongside *The Duchess and the Dragon Dentist* and *Kissed by a Cowboy Named Kevin*—it was exactly the kind of accessible, entertaining showcase that would draw browsers inside rather than test their literary credentials at the door.

Even better had been his response when she'd entered the store to acknowledge his change. No defensiveness, no justification—just honest curiosity about whether he'd gotten it right, and what looked like genuine pleasure when she'd admitted he had.

"Danielle!" Aimee Young appeared at her elbow with a warm smile, order pad in hand and the kind of energy that suggested she'd been caffeinated to perfection. "You look particularly pleased with yourself today."

"Do I?" Danielle slid into an empty booth by the window that offered a perfect view of Main Street's afternoon bustle. She supposed she did feel pleased—there was something deeply satisfying about being proven right, especially when the person who'd initially disagreed had been gracious enough to admit it.

"Well, you're not the only one in a good mood around here. That bookstore's been buzzing with activity since the window display changed." Aimee leaned against the table conspiratorially. "Mrs Patterson told me she bought three books yesterday— first time in years she's tried anything outside her usual romance series. All because the new arrangement made her curious."

"That's wonderful," Danielle said, and meant it. The goal hadn't been to prove herself right; it had been to help the bookstore actually serve its community better.

"Course, word around town is that someone gave young Mr Jones some very pointed feedback about his marketing strategy." Aimee's eyes sparkled with barely contained curiosity. "Someone with strong opinions about accessibility and customer engagement."

Before Danielle could craft a response that wouldn't be an outright admission, the bell chimed again. She glanced up automatically and felt her pulse quicken as Darius Jones entered the diner, scanning the crowd with those dark eyes that had been occupying more of her thoughts than she cared to admit.

Today he wore a navy button-down with the sleeves rolled back, and when he spotted her across the restaurant, his face lit up with what looked like genuine pleasure. He made his way directly to her table, weaving between servers and other diners with purpose.

"Mind if I join you?" he asked, one hand resting on the back of the chair across from her. "I was hoping I might run into you again."

The directness of the statement sent heat up her neck. "Of course," she managed, gesturing to the empty seat.

Aimee's eyebrows rose with obvious delight at this development. "Well, isn't this interesting. What can I get you, Darius?"

"Coffee, please. And I'll have whatever she's having," he said, settling into the booth.

"I haven't ordered yet," Danielle pointed out.

"Then I'll have whatever you decide on. I trust your judgment."

The comment landed with more weight than it should have, given that they were talking about lunch orders. But something in his tone suggested he meant more than just food choices.

"I'll give you two a few minutes to look at the menu," Aimee said with a knowing smile before finally moving away to tend to other customers.

Darius leaned forward slightly, his attention focused entirely on Danielle.

"I wanted to thank you again," he said. "Not just for the display suggestion, but for the way you approached it. You could have just complained to other people about my terrible marketing, but instead you told me directly what wasn't working."

"Most people don't appreciate direct feedback," Danielle replied, studying his face for any sign that his gratitude was purely professional courtesy.

"Most people are more concerned with being right than being effective." His smile was rueful. "I spent three months wondering why foot traffic was so low, but I was too proud to consider that my approach might be the problem."

"And now?"

"Now I'm discovering that admitting you're wrong can be surprisingly liberating." He paused as Aimee delivered their coffee. "Mrs Patterson told me yesterday that my old display made her feel like she wasn't smart enough to shop there. That was a wake-up call."

Danielle felt something warm settle in her chest at his honesty. "What made you decide to change it so completely? You could have just added one or two approachable titles."

"Because half-measures would have been missing the point." He took a sip of coffee, considering his words. "You weren't just critiquing my book choices—you were pointing out that I was prioritizing my own intellectual image over actually serving customers. That required a complete shift in thinking, not just minor adjustments."

The conversation was interrupted by Aimee delivering their lunch—chicken salad sandwiches with a side of Rochelle's famous red potato fries that neither of them had specifically ordered but both seemed pleased to receive.

"So," Darius said as they began eating, "tell me about yourself. I realize I know you have strong opinions about bookstore marketing, but not much else."

"What would you like to know?"

"Everything. What you do for work, what you read, what brought you to Sweetgum, why you cared enough about my display to start an argument with a complete stranger."

The genuine curiosity in his voice made her pulse quicken. When was the last time someone had asked about her life with such obvious interest?

"I was born here, and I'm a data analyst," she began, then found herself explaining more than she usually did about her work—how she found stories in numbers.

"What about you? What made you come back to Sweetgum to run a bookstore?" she asked.

"Long story," he said, but proceeded to tell it anyway—his history degree, the opportunity in Atlanta he'd turned down, his love of local stories and his struggle to find his place in a changing world.

As they talked, Danielle found herself noting details she hadn't caught during their previous interactions: the way he listened with complete attention, how his eyes lit up when discussing books he loved, the self-deprecating humor he used when admitting his mistakes. There was depth there, and genuine curiosity about other people's experiences.

"Can I ask you something?" Darius said as they finished eating.

"Sure."

"That first day, when you challenged my display—what made you decide to say something? Most people would have just walked away."

Danielle considered the question, trying to identify what had compelled her to engage. "I think I was frustrated by the waste of it. You clearly cared about books, about literature, but your approach was keeping people away from something you loved. It seemed like such a missed opportunity."

"So you were trying to help, not just criticize."

"Both, maybe. I was definitely annoyed by the pretentiousness. But yes, I could see the potential for something better."

"I'm glad you said something. Even if it stung at the time." His smile was warm and genuine. "Though I have to admit, I've been curious about your reading preferences. What books would you put in that window if it were your store?"

The question launched them into a discussion about guilty pleasures versus literary merit, about the books that had shaped them and the ones they recommended to friends. Danielle found herself defending romance novels while Darius made a case for the emotional complexity of science fiction, and somehow they both ended up laughing about their secret appreciation for trashy thrillers.

"I should probably get back to work," Danielle said eventually, though she made no move to leave the booth.

"Probably," he agreed, though he seemed equally reluctant to end the conversation.

"This was nice," she said, then felt heat creep up her neck at how inadequate the word sounded.

"It was. And I hope we can do it again." He hesitated, then seemed to make a decision. "Would you like to have dinner sometime? Somewhere we can continue this conversation without Aimee taking notes for the local gossip network?"

The invitation sent a flutter of excitement through her chest, followed immediately by the memory of her anticipation about the pen-pal program. Two different kinds of connection, both promising something she'd been craving.

"I'd like that," she heard herself saying.

"Saturday? I know a place in the next town over that has excellent food and minimal surveillance potential."

"Saturday sounds perfect."

As they walked out of the diner together, Danielle felt like she was stepping into something new and uncertain. The rational part of her mind reminded her about Evergreen's letter waiting at the library, about the safety of anonymous connection. But the rest of her was focused on the way Darius held the door for her, the warmth in his eyes when he smiled, and the anticipation of continuing their conversation over dinner.

Maybe she didn't have to choose between meaningful connection and romantic possibility. Maybe, for once, the universe was offering her both.

The afternoon stretched ahead with new questions and the comfortable realization that she was looking forward to finding answers to all of them.

CHAPTER EIGHT

*D*arius arrived at the Sweetgum Community Center Saturday morning with a box of books under one arm and a folding table balanced against his shoulder, questioning for the third time how he'd been talked into this. The annual Fall Festival planning committee had somehow roped him into manning a literacy booth, despite his protests that he was still learning the ropes of small-town community involvement.

At least the morning event would be over by early afternoon, leaving him time to prepare for his dinner with Danielle. The thought sent a flutter of anticipation through his chest—their first date, away from the watchful eyes of Sweetgum's unofficial surveillance network.

The morning air carried the crisp promise of autumn, and the community center's parking lot was already bustling with volunteers unloading supplies from cars and trucks. He recognized several faces from the bookstore—Mrs Patterson directing someone toward the handicap entrance, the teenagers from last week's graphic novel discussion helping an elderly man with a heavy box.

"Need a hand with that?"

He turned to find Danielle approaching with her own armload of supplies—what looked like poster boards, markers, and a folding banner that seemed determined to escape her grip. She wore dark jeans and a fitted burgundy sweater that brought out the warmth in her eyes, and her curls were pulled back in a ponytail that made him notice the graceful line of her neck.

"I've got it," he said, then immediately reconsidered as the table started to slip. "Actually, yes. Thank you."

She steadied the table while he repositioned his grip, bringing them close enough that he caught a hint of her perfume—something light and floral that made him suddenly aware of how early he'd gotten up to make sure he looked presentable for this event.

"What are the odds we'd end up working the same volunteer shift?" she asked with a slight smile that suggested she might not be entirely surprised by the coincidence.

"What are the odds we'd end up working the same volunteer shift?" she asked with a slight smile that suggested she might not be entirely surprised by the coincidence.

"In Sweetgum? Pretty high, I'd guess." He gestured toward her supplies with his free hand. "What's your noble cause?"

"Voter registration. Apparently I'm the only person under thirty they could find who wasn't already committed to something else." She readjusted her grip on the poster boards. "Though between you and me, I think Mrs Williams had something to do with our booth assignments."

"You think she's matchmaking?"

"I think she's been matchmaking since we had lunch at Rochelle's." Danielle glanced at him with amusement. "Mrs Williams has a reputation for bringing people together, one way or another."

"Well, at least we know her heart's in the right place." He

shifted his grip on the box. "And I can't complain about working alongside someone who actually knows how to make civic engagement look appealing."

"Speaking of which, I'm looking forward to our dinner tonight—somewhere we can talk without volunteer duties as a distraction."

The reminder of their evening plans sent warmth through his chest. "Me too. Though I have to admit, I'm a little nervous about taking you somewhere that meets your restaurant standards."

"Don't be. I'm not that picky—I just appreciate places that put thought into their atmosphere as well as their food."

They walked into the community center together, and Darius found himself oddly pleased by the coincidence of their assignment, even if it had been orchestrated by well-meaning community members. Working together this morning felt like a pleasant prelude to their evening plans.

Inside, the main hall buzzed with organized chaos as volunteers set up booths for everything from the historical society to the garden club. Tables lined the perimeter while local businesses arranged displays in the center. The smell of coffee and fresh donuts from the Roasted Beans Coffee Spot hospitality station mingled with the scent of the autumn decorations that volunteers were hanging from every available surface.

Mrs Williams stood in the center of it all with a clipboard, directing traffic with the efficiency of someone who'd organized dozens of such events over the years. She wore a bright orange sweater that made her silver hair shine, and her energy level suggested she'd been up since dawn coordinating details.

"Danielle, Darius!" she called out, spotting them across the room. "Perfect timing. I've got you two set up right next to each other—voter registration and literacy promotion go hand in hand, don't you think?"

Darius caught Danielle's eye and saw his own amusement reflected there. "Convenient," she murmured under her breath.

"Very," he agreed, following Mrs Williams to their assigned corner near the windows that overlooked the community center's small garden.

"Now, I've put you next to the historical society booth on one side and the library's children's programming table on the other," Mrs Williams continued, clearly pleased with her arrangements. "Thought you might appreciate being surrounded by fellow book lovers."

The next hour was spent in companionable setup— arranging tables, hanging banners, organizing materials. Darius found himself stealing glances at Danielle as she worked, noting the efficient way she organized her voter registration forms and the careful attention she paid to making her display welcoming rather than bureaucratic. She'd brought tablecloths, colorful pens, and small American flag decorations that transformed what could have been a dry civic duty into something that looked approachable and even festive.

"Nice touch," he said, nodding toward the small bowl of chocolate candy she'd placed at the front of her table. "Civic duty with a sweet reward."

"Learned it from my sister Chrysta. She says you catch more flies with honey than with lectures about democratic participation." Danielle stepped back to survey her work, hands on her hips in a gesture of satisfaction. "Though between you and me, I think people should register to vote because it matters, not because they get a mini chocolate bar."

"But the mini chocolate doesn't hurt."

"Exactly." She turned to examine his setup—a collection of book recommendations organized by age group, along with pamphlets about the library's programs and reading challenges. Everything was neatly arranged and clearly labeled, but somehow lacked the warmth of her display. "Very organized. Very... professional."

He caught the slight tease in her tone and felt his defenses start to rise before remembering their recent conversations about meeting people where they were. "But?"

"No but. It's good. Just maybe a little..." She gestured vaguely, searching for the right word.

"Intimidating?" he suggested wryly.

"I was going to say 'institutional,' but intimidating works too." Her smile took the sting out of the criticism. "Where's the book that made you fall in love with reading? The one that made you decide words were magic?"

The question caught him off guard. He'd focused so much on showcasing literary merit and educational value that he'd forgotten about passion, about the personal connection that made books matter in the first place. His display looked like something from a library conference, not something that would make a reluctant reader curious about stories.

"That's... actually a really insightful point." He rummaged through his box and pulled out a battered paperback copy of *Captain Whiskers and the Treasure of Magical Island*. "This was my gateway drug. Read it when I was eight and decided that words could build entire worlds full of adventure."

"Now we're talking." Danielle helped him position the book prominently on his table, right next to his professionally printed sign. "See? Much more inviting than 'Recommended Reading by Age Group.' This says 'I'm a real person who discovered the magic of stories as a kid.'"

Their hands brushed as they adjusted the display, and Darius felt that same electric awareness that had marked their encounter at the diner. But this time, instead of defensive sparring, they were collaborating. Building something together that was better than what either of them had created alone.

The doors opened to the public at ten, and a steady stream of families began filtering through the main hall. Darius watched Danielle work, impressed by how she engaged with people—asking about their interests, explaining the voting process without condescension, making even the most civic-minded tasks feel approachable and important.

When a teenage girl approached his table with obvious reluctance, clearly dragged there by her mother, Darius found himself channeling Danielle's approach.

"Let me guess," he said with a conspiratorial smile. "Someone told you reading is good for you and you should find something educational?"

The girl's eyes widened with surprise. "Yeah. Mom says I need to read more classics because I'm taking AP English next year."

Instead of reaching for his prepared list of recommended titles, Darius picked up a graphic novel about teenage superheroes saving the world through strategic thinking and teamwork. "What if we started with something that proves reading can be fun, and then worked our way up to the stuff your teacher assigns?"

Her face lit up as she flipped through the colorful pages. "This looks cool. Like, actually cool, not adult-pretending-to-understand-teenagers cool."

"I promise it's genuinely cool. And if you like it, I've got five more in the series." He handed her a bookmark with the bookstore's information. "Plus, once you're hooked on stories, the classics won't feel like homework anymore. They'll just be older stories with different kinds of artwork."

After she left with her book and a promise to visit the store, Darius caught Danielle watching him with an expression of unmistakable approval.

"What?" he asked.

"Nothing. Just... that was perfectly done. You met her where she was instead of where her mother thought she should be."

"I had a good teacher this week," he said quietly, holding her gaze long enough to see understanding flicker in her eyes.

Before she could respond, a commotion at the entrance drew their attention. The hit-and-run squad had arrived in formation—Mrs Andrews, Mrs Bridges, and Mrs Craskin, all wearing matching festival t-shirts and determined expressions that suggested they were on a mission that went beyond simple event attendance.

"Incoming," Danielle murmured with barely concealed amusement, settling herself behind her voter registration table like someone preparing for friendly combat.

The three women made a beeline for their corner, clearly having planned their approach in advance.

"Danielle, dear," Mrs Andrews said without preamble, "we need to discuss your registration materials. Very professional, very thorough, but where are the candidate information sheets?"

While Danielle patiently explained the nonpartisan nature of voter registration, Mrs Bridges turned her attention to Darius with the focused intensity of someone conducting an investigation.

"Young man, we've been hearing wonderful things about your new window display. Much more approachable than that stuffy classics showcase you had before."

Heat crept up Darius's neck. "Thank you. I had some helpful feedback."

Mrs Craskin's eyes sparkled with mischief as she glanced between him and Danielle. "Helpful feedback indeed. Nothing like a spirited conversation between young people to spark positive changes. And continued collaboration, it seems."

"We're just volunteering together," Danielle said quickly.

"Of course you are," Mrs Andrews replied with knowing

satisfaction. "And I'm sure you'll find plenty more opportunities to volunteer together in the future."

After they moved on to interrogate other volunteers, Danielle shook her head with rueful amusement. "They're going to have us married off by Christmas at this rate."

"Does that bother you?" Darius asked, then immediately worried he'd been too direct.

"The matchmaking? Or the marriage speculation?"

"Either. Both."

She considered the question while straightening her voter registration forms. "I think I mind the assumption that we can't just be friends or colleagues without it being romantic. But I don't mind people hoping we might be happy together."

The honesty in her answer made his chest warm. "I feel the same way. Though I have to admit, I'm hoping tonight goes well enough that their speculation isn't entirely off base."

Her smile in response was worth whatever gossip the hit-and-run squad might generate.

The afternoon flew by in a blur of voter registrations and book recommendations, punctuated by ongoing conversation between their tables. By two o'clock, when the event wound down and volunteers began packing up their displays, Darius realized he'd enjoyed himself more than he had at any social gathering in months.

"Not bad for our first community service collaboration," Danielle said as they packed up their materials.

"Assuming it won't be our last," he replied, loading books back into his box.

"Well, that depends on how dinner goes tonight," she said with a teasing smile that made his pulse quicken.

"No pressure at all," he said dryly.

As they walked out of the community center together, Darius found himself looking forward to the evening ahead with an anticipation that felt both nerve-wracking and exciting.

In just a few hours, they'd be sitting across from each other at a restaurant, no community event to distract them, no volunteer duties to hide behind—just two people getting to know each other over good food and honest conversation.

He couldn't wait.

CHAPTER NINE

$\mathcal{D}$anielle sat at her vanity mirror Saturday evening, fixing her hair with hands that trembled slightly with nervous excitement. In twenty minutes, Darius would pick her up for their first real date—dinner at a small Italian restaurant in Peachwood, the next town over, far enough from Sweetgum's watchful eyes to allow for uninterrupted conversation.

The community service event that morning had shown her a different side of him entirely. Gone was the defensive intellectual who'd bristled at her criticism of his window display. Instead, she'd worked alongside someone who was collaborative, thoughtful, and genuinely interested in connecting people with stories they'd love rather than stories they should read.

Her phone buzzed with a text from Aleeyah:

> How are you feeling about tonight? Nervous? Excited? Both?

> Both

Danielle typed back.

> He was really different today during the
> community event. More... open. Less defensive
> about his choices.

Aleeyah responded,

> Character development in real time. I love it.
> Have fun tonight!

As Danielle put the finishing touches on her appearance—dark jeans, a soft blue sweater that brought out the brown in her eyes, and just enough makeup to feel polished without trying too hard,—Danielle found her thoughts drifting to the letter she'd received from Evergreen that morning.

His latest correspondence had arrived with the usual careful handwriting and thoughtful observations, but something about it felt different this time. More personal, perhaps. He'd written about learning to take feedback gracefully, about discovering that the people who challenged his assumptions often cared more than those who simply nodded along.

The timing felt oddly coincidental, given her evolving feelings about Darius. But surely that was all it was—coincidence. Sweetgum might be small, but not so small that only one person could be having revelations about intellectual humility and meaningful connection.

A soft knock at her door interrupted her contemplation. She glanced at the clock—seven on the dot. Punctual, she noted with approval, grabbing her purse and jacket.

When she opened the door, Darius stood there looking handsome in dark jeans and a navy button-down that made his eyes seem even more intense than usual. He held a small bouquet of autumn flowers—nothing too elaborate, but thoughtful enough to suggest he'd put care into the gesture.

"These are lovely," she said, accepting the flowers with genuine pleasure. "Let me just put them in water."

"No rush. Our reservation isn't until seven-thirty."

As she arranged the flowers in a vase, she was aware of him standing in her small living room, probably taking in the built-in bookshelves that lined one wall, the reading chair positioned by the window, the stack of notebooks on her coffee table.

"Nice place," he said when she returned. "I can see why you chose that spot for your reading chair—perfect light."

"It's where I do most of my thinking," she admitted. "And my writing."

His eyes lit up with interest. "You write? What kind of writing?"

"Poetry, mostly. And some personal essays." She felt heat creep up her neck. "Nothing published or anything. Just... thoughts that need to come out in more than spreadsheet form."

"That's wonderful. I'd love to read some of your work some-time, if you're comfortable sharing." His enthusiasm seemed genuine, not polite. "I write too—historical fiction, mostly. Or I try to, anyway. It's been harder since I moved back, finding the time and headspace."

"What kind of historical fiction?"

"Stories about ordinary people during extraordinary times. How regular folks navigated major historical changes." He gestured toward her notebooks. "But poetry—that takes a different kind of courage. Distilling emotion and observation into something that resonates with strangers."

The understanding in his voice made her pulse quicken. When was the last time someone had recognized writing as an act of courage rather than just a hobby?

THE DRIVE to Bella Vista took twenty minutes through winding country roads lined with trees just beginning to turn. They talked easily about the morning's event, comparing notes on the different people they'd helped and laughing about the hit-and-run squad's obvious matchmaking attempts.

"Mrs Bridges actually asked me if I thought you were 'relationship material,'" Darius said as they pulled into the restaurant's parking lot. "I told her that was something I intended to find out for myself."

"Very diplomatic. What did she say to that?" she laughed.

"That I was a smart young man who knew a good thing when he saw it." His smile was rueful. "I'm beginning to understand that privacy is a luxury in small towns."

"The price of community, I suppose. Everyone cares about everyone else's business because everyone genuinely cares about everyone else."

Bella Vista turned out to be exactly the kind of place Danielle appreciated—family-owned, with mismatched tables and the kind of atmosphere that prioritized good food and genuine hospitality over fancy presentation. The owner, an elderly Italian woman named Rosa, greeted them warmly and led them to a corner table lit by candles and overlooking a small garden.

"This is perfect," Danielle said, settling into her chair and admiring the intimate setting. "How did you find this place?"

"My grandmother's recommendation. She and my grandfather used to come here for special occasions." He paused, looking slightly embarrassed. "I hope it doesn't seem presumptuous, choosing somewhere with romantic associations."

The honesty in his admission made her pulse quicken. "Not presumptuous. Sweet."

As they perused the menu and ordered drinks, Danielle found herself studying Darius in the soft candlelight. Away from the bookstore and the community center, he seemed more relaxed, less guarded. The defensive tension she'd noticed during their first encounter had been replaced by something warmer, more open.

"Can I ask you something?" she said after the server had taken their dinner orders.

"Anything."

"I know I asked you before, but what made you decide to come back to Sweetgum? Really, I mean. Beyond the family obligations."

He was quiet for a moment, swirling drink in his glass as he considered the question. "I think I was tired of feeling anonymous. In Atlanta, I would have been one researcher among hundreds, processing other people's discoveries, contributing to knowledge in ways that felt important but impersonal." He looked up at her. "Here, I get to help Mrs Patterson discover authors she's never tried, or watch a teenager realize that graphic novels count as real reading. The impact is smaller in scope, but more immediate. Personal."

"That's beautiful," she said softly. "And much more honest than most people are about their career choices."

The sentiment reminded her of something Evergreen had written about finding meaning in work that connected directly with people's lives. But she pushed the thought aside—surely lots of people felt that way about their career choices.

"What about you?" Darius continued. "Have you always wanted to work with data, or did you fall into it?"

Danielle found herself explaining her journey from English literature to data analysis, how she'd been drawn to finding stories hidden in numbers, patterns that revealed human behavior and motivation. As she talked, she noticed the way he listened—completely engaged, asking thoughtful follow-up questions that showed he was genuinely interested in understanding her perspective.

"So you're a storyteller either way," he observed. "Whether it's through poetry or spreadsheets."

"I never thought of it that way, but yes. I suppose I am."

Their food arrived—perfectly prepared pasta with rich

sauces that demanded full attention—but somehow they managed to keep talking between bites. The conversation flowed naturally from work to family to books they'd loved, revealing layers of compatibility that went beyond their shared interest in literature.

"I have to ask," Danielle said as they shared a dessert of tiramisu, "what's your guilty reading pleasure? The book you'd never recommend to customers but secretly love?"

Darius laughed, ducking his head slightly. "Promise you won't judge me?"

"I promise."

"Romance novels. Specifically, historical romance with completely ridiculous titles like 'The Duke's Forbidden Passion' or 'Love in the Time of Corsets.' I know they're formulaic, but there's something comforting about stories where you know everything will work out in the end."

"That's not guilty at all," Danielle said warmly. "That's knowing what feeds your soul. I do the same thing with cozy mysteries—give me a small English village with an amateur detective and a murder that gets solved over tea and I'm completely happy."

"See, that's what I love about this conversation. No judgment, just genuine interest in what makes each other tick."

As the evening progressed, Danielle found herself noting small details that felt familiar: the way Darius chose his words carefully when discussing something important, his tendency to ask thoughtful questions rather than simply waiting for his turn to talk, his genuine curiosity about her perspective on things. The similarities to her anonymous correspondent were striking, but not definitive enough to draw conclusions.

"I should probably confess something," Darius said as they lingered over coffee, clearly reluctant to end the evening. "I was nervous about tonight. Not just first-date nerves, but worried that we might not have as much in common as I hoped."

"And now?"

"Now I'm wondering why I was worried. This has been the best conversation I've had in... well, in a very long time." He paused, his expression growing thoughtful. "Actually, I've been exchanging letters with someone recently—anonymously, through Mrs Williams' program—and our written conversations have been really meaningful. But this feels different. Better. More complete."

Danielle's pulse quickened at the mention of letters, but she kept her expression neutral. "The pen-pal program? I've heard good things about it."

"It's been surprisingly rewarding. My correspondent writes beautifully about finding meaning in everyday work, about the courage it takes to really connect with people." He looked at her with warm eyes. "But sitting here with you, I'm realizing that no amount of meaningful correspondence can compare to actually being with someone you care about."

The words sent a flutter through her chest—both at the compliment and at the uncanny echo of thoughts she'd been having about her own anonymous exchange. But she simply smiled and said, "I'm glad you feel that way."

As they drove back to Sweetgum, the car filled with comfortable conversation and the promise of future evenings together, Danielle found herself in an odd position. She was falling for Darius—that much was clear from the way her heart raced when he laughed, the way she hung on his every word, the anticipation she felt about seeing him again. But she was also growing more intrigued by her correspondence with Evergreen, whose letters revealed a depth and thoughtfulness that made her eager for each new exchange.

The possibility that they might be the same person flickered through her mind, but she dismissed it as wishful thinking. The universe wasn't usually that generous with its coincidences.

When they reached her apartment, Darius walked her to the

door like a proper gentleman, but she could feel the tension building between them with each step. The evening had been perfect, and neither seemed ready for it to end.

"I had a wonderful time tonight," she said, turning to face him in the soft glow of her porch light.

"So did I." His voice was lower than usual, rougher around the edges. "Would you like to do it again sometime?"

"I'd love to."

They stood there for a moment, the air between them charged with possibility. Danielle could feel her heart hammering against her ribs as Darius stepped closer, close enough that she could catch the scent of his cologne mixed with the crisp autumn air.

"Danielle," he said softly, her name sounding different on his lips than it ever had before—more intimate, more precious.

When he reached up to cup her face, his thumb brushing across her cheek with infinite gentleness, she felt her breath catch. His eyes searched hers in the golden porch light, asking a question she answered by lifting her face toward him.

The first brush of his lips against hers was tentative, almost reverent, as if he was afraid she might disappear. But when she sighed and melted into him, her hands fisting in the front of his shirt, he deepened the kiss with a passion that made her knees weak.

His lips were warm and sure, moving against hers with a tenderness that spoke of careful restraint and barely controlled desire. She could taste the drink they'd shared, could feel the slight tremor in his hands as they framed her face, could hear the soft sound he made when she kissed him back with equal fervor.

Time seemed to stop on her small porch, the world narrowing to nothing but the feeling of his mouth on hers, the solid warmth of his body, the way he kissed her like she was something rare and wonderful that he'd been searching for his entire life.

When they finally broke apart, both breathing hard, he rested his forehead against hers.

"I've been wanting to do that all evening," he admitted, his voice barely above a whisper.

"I've been hoping you would," she replied, surprised by her own boldness.

The smile that spread across his face was radiant, transforming his already handsome features into something that made her heart skip entirely. "I should go," he said, though he made no move to step away from her.

"You should," she agreed, though she tightened her grip on his shirt.

He pressed one more soft kiss to her lips, then another to her forehead, before finally stepping back. "Sweet dreams, Danielle."

As she watched him drive away, Danielle touched her lips, still feeling the warmth of his kiss. Her whole body was humming with electricity, and she felt like she was standing at the beginning of something beautiful and terrifying and absolutely worth whatever came next.

CHAPTER TEN

$\mathcal{D}$arius woke up Sunday morning with a smile he couldn't suppress, the memory of Saturday night's perfect first date—and that incredible goodnight kiss—still sending warmth through his chest. He lay in bed for a few extra minutes, replaying every moment: the way Danielle had looked in that blue sweater, how easily their conversation had flowed over dinner, the soft sound she'd made when he'd finally kissed her on her porch.

His phone buzzed with a text from Chris:

> My grandmother wanted me to remind you that letter pickup is available anytime after 2 PM today.

The message sent a familiar flutter through his chest, though it was different now, complicated by his growing feelings for Danielle. Maplewood Muse's latest letter was waiting, and her previous response had left him with more questions than answers. Her mention of working alongside someone she'd initially clashed with, her observations about first impressions versus deeper character—the parallels to his own situation with Danielle were becoming harder to dismiss as coincidence.

But he was probably reading too much into it. Sweetgum might be small, but surely more than one person was capable of having complex thoughts about human nature and personal growth.

He stretched, finally forcing himself out of bed and into his usual Sunday morning routine. Coffee first, then a quick shower before heading downstairs to check on the bookstore and handle any weekend tasks that needed attention.

The morning sunlight streaming through his apartment windows felt brighter than usual, everything touched with the golden glow of new possibility. Last night had confirmed what he'd been hoping—that his initial impression of Danielle as a challenging adversary had been completely wrong. She was thoughtful, funny, passionate about things that mattered, and somehow saw past his defensive pretenses to the person he actually wanted to be.

The way she'd melted into that kiss, the soft sigh she'd made when he'd cupped her face, the way she'd gripped his shirt like she was afraid he might disappear—it had all felt like coming home to something he hadn't even known he was missing.

His phone rang, interrupting his pleasant memories. His grandmother's name appeared on the screen.

"Good morning, Grandma," he answered, settling into his kitchen chair with his coffee.

"Good morning, dear. I hope I'm not calling too early." Her voice carried that particular note of barely contained curiosity that meant she'd heard something interesting. "I ran into Mrs Chen at the early service, and she mentioned seeing you and that lovely Danielle Jacobs at Bella Vista last night."

Darius felt heat creep up his neck. He'd known that choosing a restaurant twenty minutes away wouldn't guarantee complete privacy, but he'd hoped for at least a day before the news made it back to Sweetgum's unofficial intelligence network.

"We had dinner," he confirmed, aiming for casual.

"How wonderful! And how did it go?"

"Very well." Despite his embarrassment at being the subject of small-town gossip, he couldn't keep the smile out of his voice. "She's... she's really special, Grandma."

"I could have told you that weeks ago, dear. That young woman has a good head on her shoulders and isn't afraid to speak her mind when something matters to her. She reminds me of myself at that age, actually. Your grandfather always said he fell for me because I challenged him to be better than he thought he could be." There was a pause, and he could practically hear her thinking. "Are you planning to see her again?"

"I hope so. We didn't make specific plans, but..." He trailed off, realizing he was probably revealing more than he intended to. "Yes, I think we'll see each other again."

"Good. Your grandfather will be pleased—he's been worried you were spending too much time alone with your books and your writing."

After they hung up, Darius found himself restless with anticipation and nervous energy. The morning stretched ahead with no specific plans beyond collecting his letter from Maplewood Muse, and he found himself wondering what Danielle was doing, whether she was thinking about their evening together, when it would be appropriate to call or text her.

He forced himself to focus on practical tasks—updating inventory records, organizing the storage room, reviewing the week's special orders. But his thoughts kept drifting to the feel of Danielle's lips against his, the way she'd looked at him like he was someone worth knowing, the promise he'd heard in her voice when she'd said she'd like to see him again.

At two-fifteen, he walked to the library, enjoying the crisp autumn air and the quiet Sunday afternoon atmosphere. Main

Street was mostly deserted except for families heading home from church and a few early fall tourists admiring the changing leaves.

Mrs Williams was at the circulation desk when he entered, and her face lit up with obvious delight when she saw him.

"Darius! Perfect timing. I have your letter right here." She handed over the familiar envelope with ceremony. "I have to say, the early feedback from the pen-pal program has been extraordinary. People are really connecting in ways I hoped for but didn't dare expect."

"That's wonderful," Darius said, tucking the letter into his jacket pocket. He found himself curious about the other matches, wondering if anyone else was experiencing the kind of meaningful correspondence he'd been sharing with Maplewood Muse.

"Some pairs are becoming genuine friends," Mrs Williams continued, clearly pleased with her matchmaking success. "Others seem to be developing even deeper connections. It's beautiful to witness."

"I imagine some connections are deeper than others," Darius said carefully.

"Oh, absolutely. Some correspondences are lovely but casual —shared interests, friendly conversation about books and local happenings. Others..." She paused with a meaningful look that suggested she knew more than she was saying. "Others seem to be touching something more profound. Hearts recognizing hearts across the anonymity, you might say."

The comment sent a flutter of anticipation through his chest. Back in his apartment, Darius settled into his reading chair and opened Maplewood Muse's letter with hands that weren't entirely steady.

Dear Evergreen,

I've been thinking about our recent correspondence and how much it's meant to me during a time of uncertainty and change. Your letters have become the highlight of my week, and I find myself looking forward to them with an anticipation that goes beyond simple intellectual curiosity.

You asked about developing feelings for someone who started as an intellectual adversary, and I find myself in the strange position of possibly experiencing exactly that. There's someone in my life who initially frustrated me with their rigid thinking, but who's proven to be thoughtful, vulnerable, and surprisingly open to growth. Our recent interactions have revealed depths I hadn't expected, and I find myself drawn to them in ways that feel both exciting and terrifying.

But here's what puzzles me: the more I get to know this person, the more they remind me of you. Not in obvious ways, but in their passion for literature, their willingness to examine their own assumptions, their genuine desire to connect with others through shared stories. The timing of our respective revelations about intellectual humility feels too coincidental to ignore.

I know this might sound presumptuous, but I can't shake the feeling that the universe might be orchestrating something here. That perhaps our anonymous correspondence and my growing real-world connection might be two sides of the same beautiful coin.

What would you think about the possibility of meeting? Not necessarily revealing our identities immediately, but perhaps arranging to encounter each other in a public space where we might recognize something familiar in each other's presence?

I understand if this seems too forward, and I don't want to complicate something that's been so meaningful in its current form. But I also can't ignore the growing conviction that meaningful connections are rare enough that when we find them, we should be brave about pursuing them.

Yours in curiosity and hope,
Maplewood Muse

P.S. I hope your evening plans, whatever they were, brought you the kind of joy and connection you deserve. Something tells me you're someone who gives so much to others that you sometimes forget to seek happiness for yourself.

Darius read the letter three times, his heart racing with each pass. The timing, the specific details about intellectual adversaries and growth, her mention of someone who reminded her of him—it was all pointing toward a conclusion that seemed too perfect to be real.

Could Maplewood Muse actually be Danielle? The woman whose letters had been feeding his soul for weeks and the woman whose kiss had set his world on fire last night—could they possibly be the same person?

His hands shook slightly as he pulled out paper and began composing his response. If his growing suspicion was correct, then this letter might be the key to discovering whether the universe really was as generous with its coincidences as it seemed.

Dear Maplewood Muse,

Your letter arrived at a moment when I needed to hear exactly those words. I've been grappling with similar questions about connection and timing, about whether it's possible to fall for someone in two different ways simultaneously.

The person who challenged my approach to sharing literature has become increasingly important to me. What started as defensive sparring has evolved into something I treasure—first respect for their insights, then appreciation for their passion, and now something deeper that I'm still learning to name.

Like you, I've been struck by the parallels between my real-world experiences and our correspondence. The timing of our mutual revelations, the similar struggles with intellectual pride, the shared journey toward more authentic connection—it feels like more than coincidence.

I would very much like to meet you, though I'll admit the prospect terrifies me as much as it excites me. What if our written connection doesn't translate to person-to-person compatibility? What if the mystery is more appealing than the reality?

But then I think about your letters, about the

depth and warmth and intelligence that comes through in every line, and I realize that anyone capable of such thoughtful correspondence must be worth knowing in person.

Would you be interested in meeting at the bookstore on Main Street this Thursday evening around six? It's a place that holds significance for me—where I've been learning to share my love of literature more generously, largely thanks to someone who wasn't afraid to challenge my assumptions.

If you're comfortable with it, we could arrange to "accidentally" encounter each other there. If nothing else, we'll have books to talk about if the conversation falters.

Eagerly awaiting your thoughts,
Evergreen

P.S. My evening plans yesterday exceeded all expectations and left me feeling more hopeful about the future than I have in years. Thank you for your kind wishes— they mean more than you know.

As he sealed the envelope, Darius felt like he was standing at the edge of something momentous. If Maplewood Muse was indeed Danielle, then Thursday evening would bring either the most romantic revelation of his life or the most awkward misunderstanding in small-town history.

Either way, he couldn't wait to find out.

He looked around his apartment—at the books that lined his shelves, the writing desk where he'd crafted so many letters to his anonymous correspondent, the reading chair where he'd fallen in love with Maplewood Muse's words before he'd fallen in love with Danielle's kiss.

If they were the same person, then every letter he'd written had been honest, every feeling he'd shared had been true. He'd been courting the same woman in two different ways, falling for her mind through correspondence and her heart through shared glances and stolen kisses.

The thought should have been overwhelming, but instead it filled him with a sense of rightness he'd never experienced before. Sometimes the best stories were the ones that surprised you by weaving together threads you hadn't even realized were part of the same tapestry.

And if he was right about Maplewood Muse's identity, then his story with Danielle was about to become even more beautiful than he'd dared to hope.

Thursday couldn't come soon enough.

CHAPTER ELEVEN

Danielle practically floated into work Monday morning, still glowing from Saturday night's perfect dinner with Darius. The weekend had passed in a pleasant haze of replaying every moment—his vulnerability about wanting to make a meaningful difference, his genuine interest in her poetry writing, the way he'd listened when she'd shared her struggles with feeling invisible in her own life.

And that kiss. She touched her lips unconsciously, still feeling the warmth of his mouth against hers, the gentle way he'd cupped her face, the soft sound he'd made when she'd kissed him back with equal fervor.

"Someone's looking happy," observed her coworker Janet, glancing up from her computer screen with obvious curiosity. "Good weekend?"

"Very good weekend," Danielle admitted, settling at her desk with a smile she couldn't quite suppress.

She tried to focus on her quarterly analysis spreadsheets, but her mind kept drifting back to moments from their date: the way Darius had laughed at her observations about small-town life, how his eyes had lit up when she'd mentioned her secret poetry writing, the anticipation that had built throughout dinner as they'd discovered layer after layer of compatibility.

Her phone buzzed with a text from Chrysta:

> Aleeyah told me about your date Saturday.
> Need details. Lunch today?

Before she could respond, another text arrived from Aleeyah herself:

> How did it go?? Was he less pretentious in a romantic setting?

Danielle typed back:

> Better than expected. Much better. Will call you both later with details.

At lunch, she walked to the library with nervous energy humming through her veins, anticipating Evergreen's response to her latest letter. Chris was at the circulation desk when she entered, and he handed over her envelope with his usual friendly smile.

"My grandmother is starting to plan that reveal event she mentioned," he said conversationally as she tucked the letter into her purse. "Optional, of course, but she thinks some of the pen-pal pairs might be ready to meet in person."

"Really?" Danielle tried to keep her voice casual. "When would that be?"

"Probably in a few weeks. She wants to give people more time to develop their connections first." He grinned. "Though between you and me, I think she's enjoying the suspense too much to rush things."

Back at her desk, Danielle found a quiet corner of the break room and opened Evergreen's letter with hands that trembled slightly. As she read his words, her pulse began to race with each paragraph.

His confession about falling for someone in two different ways simultaneously felt like reading her own thoughts written in someone else's handwriting. When he wrote about the parallels between his correspondence and real-world experiences, about similar struggles with intellectual pride and growth—it was as if he was describing her exact situation with Darius.

But it was his suggestion about meeting at the bookstore Thursday evening that made her heart stop completely. The specificity of it, the confidence with which he'd chosen that location and time—it felt like something someone familiar with that space would propose.

And then there was his postscript about his evening plans exceeding expectations, written with a timing that suggested he'd penned this letter right after a significant night out. Given when she'd received it, that could only mean Saturday evening.

Her phone rang, interrupting her racing thoughts. Chrysta's name appeared on the screen.

"How was the date?" her sister asked without preamble.

"Wonderful. Confusing. I think I might be losing my mind." Danielle rubbed her temples. "Chrysta, what if I told you that my anonymous pen pal just suggested we meet at the bookstore Thursday evening, and that he mentioned having a perfect evening recently that 'exceeded all expectations'?"

"I'd say the universe has a sense of humor about romantic timing. Are you going to meet him?"

"I think I have to. Either I'm about to have the most romantic revelation of my life, or I'm about to discover I've been projecting patterns that don't exist." Danielle stared at the letter. "But the parallels are too specific to ignore anymore."

"Then you write back and say yes. And then you prepare yourself for either the best Thursday evening ever or a really interesting story to tell your grandchildren."

After they hung up, Danielle pulled out paper and began her

response, her heart hammering as she addressed each point Evergreen had raised.

Dear Evergreen,

Your letter left me staring at the page in amazement, because you've managed to put into words exactly what I've been feeling but haven't known how to express. The idea that we might both be "falling for someone in two different ways simultaneously" feels like you've been reading my thoughts.

When you write about the parallels between your correspondence and real-world experiences, about similar struggles and mutual revelations—I can barely breathe reading those words, because they describe my situation so perfectly it can't be coincidence. The timing, the specific details about intellectual adversaries becoming something deeper—either we're living remarkably parallel lives, or we're living the same life from different perspectives.

Your suggestion about meeting at the bookstore Thursday evening around six feels absolutely right. That space holds significance for me too, as a place where I've learned important lessons about meeting people where they are rather than where I think they should be. If you are who I'm beginning to suspect you might be, then that location carries even more meaning.

I understand your fear that the mystery might

be more appealing than the reality—I share that terror completely. What if our written chemistry doesn't translate? What if knowing each other's identities changes the dynamic we've built? But then I think about your letters, about the depth and warmth and intelligence in every line, and I realize that anyone capable of this kind of thoughtful correspondence must be worth knowing in whatever form that takes.

I'm also struck by your postscript about your evening plans exceeding expectations. The timing of that comment, given when I received your letter, makes me wonder if perhaps we shared more than just correspondence recently. If I'm right about who you are, then I'm even more eager for Thursday evening—not just to solve a mystery, but to discover if the person whose letters have been feeding my soul might also be the person whose company has been lighting up my world.

So yes, I'll be at the bookstore Thursday at six, probably browsing the poetry section and trying not to look as nervous as I feel. If you're someone I already know, this will either be the most romantic revelation or the most beautifully awkward encounter in recent memory.

Counting down the hours,
Maplewood Muse

P.S. Thank you for your kind wishes about my own recent evening. It was indeed wonderful—filled with the kind of conversation and connection I didn't know I was missing. If my suspicions are correct, then you already know exactly how wonderful it was.

As she sealed the envelope, Danielle felt like she was standing at the edge of a precipice. Thursday evening would either confirm her wildest romantic hope or teach her a valuable lesson about the difference between coincidence and destiny.

Either way, she couldn't wait to find out which it would be.

The afternoon dragged by with unusual slowness, every minute feeling like an hour as she anticipated Thursday's arrival. Walking past the bookstore on her way home, she caught sight of Darius through the window, helping a customer select books from his newly accessible display.

In three days, she might know for certain whether the man making her heart race and the correspondent making her think were one and the same. The possibility filled her with equal measures of excitement and terror.

Because sometimes the best love stories were the ones that surprised you by being exactly what you needed, delivered in ways you never could have predicted.

CHAPTER TWELVE

*D*arius sat in his grandparents' living room Wednesday evening, trying to focus on their conversation about the upcoming Fall Festival while his mind raced with thoughts of tomorrow's meeting. In less than twenty-four hours, he would finally come face to face with Maplewood Muse at the bookstore. The anticipation was making it impossible to concentrate on anything else.

He'd received her enthusiastic response to his meeting suggestion on Tuesday morning, and her letter had been everything he'd hoped for and more. The way she'd written about their evening plans "exceeding expectations" and her reference to sharing "more than just correspondence recently" had made the connection feel almost undeniable. But still, a part of him wondered if he was projecting patterns that weren't really there.

"You're distracted tonight, dear," his grandmother observed, setting down her knitting to study his face with the shrewd attention of someone who'd raised three children and countless grandchildren. "Everything alright with the store?"

"The store's fine. Better than fine, actually." He shifted in his chair, trying to appear more present than he felt. The window display change had continued to bring in new customers, and he'd had several conversations with browsers who mentioned feeling more welcome in the space. "I've just got some personal things on my mind."

His grandparents exchanged one of their meaningful looks —the kind that came from fifty-three years of marriage and an uncanny ability to communicate entire conversations without words. His grandfather set down his evening paper with the deliberate care of someone preparing to conduct a gentle investigation.

"Would these personal things happen to involve that lovely young woman you've been spending time with?" his grandfather asked with barely concealed amusement. "Danielle, wasn't it?"

Heat crept up Darius's neck. In a town the size of Sweetgum, his Saturday night dinner date had probably been reported to every interested party by Sunday morning. Mrs Chen had likely provided a full report to anyone who'd listen about seeing them at Bella Vista. "Partly."

"And?" his grandmother prompted gently, settling back into her chair with the patience of someone who'd perfected the art of drawing out information from reluctant family members.

Darius found himself explaining about the pen-pal program, about the thoughtful letters he'd been exchanging with someone whose perspective seemed to align perfectly with his own growing understanding of what mattered in life. He described the intellectual depth of their correspondence, the way Maplewood Muse challenged his assumptions while supporting his growth, the anticipation he felt each time a new letter arrived.

"She writes about literature and life in ways that make me think differently about both," he said, running a hand over his hair. "Her letters have become something I look forward to more than I probably should. We're supposed to meet tomorrow evening, and I'm terrified and excited in equal measure."

His grandmother's knitting needles had stopped clicking, and she was watching him with the focused attention she usually reserved for particularly complex patterns. "That sounds wonderful, dear. Anonymous correspondence can create such meaningful connections. But you seem troubled about something."

"It's complicated." Darius hesitated, then decided his grandparents had earned the right to honest communication after decades of offering unconditional support. "The timing of her letters, the things she writes about—there are coincidences that make me wonder if she might be someone I already know."

"Oh my." His grandmother's eyes lit up with understanding, and she set her knitting aside entirely. "You think it might be Danielle?"

"I don't know. Maybe." The words felt strange to voice, as if speaking his suspicion aloud might jinx the possibility. "The way she writes about encounters with someone who challenged her thinking, references to collaborative work and seeing unexpected sides of people—it sounds remarkably similar to my interactions with Danielle. The timing of everything feels too coincidental."

His grandfather leaned forward in his recliner, clearly intrigued by this romantic development. "So you're developing feelings for two different women," he summarized with the directness that had served him well in forty years of high school teaching. "Your pen pal and Danielle."

"It's more complicated than that." Darius stood and began pacing the small living room, his nervous energy too much for sitting still. "If they are the same person, then everything I've been sharing in those letters—my doubts about my approach to the bookstore, my feelings about connection and growth, my growing attraction to someone who started as an intellectual adversary—she already knows all of it."

"And how do you feel about that possibility?" his grandmother asked, her voice gentle but probing.

Darius stopped pacing and considered the question carefully. "Terrified. Excited. If it is her, then I've been falling for the same person in two different ways, and that feels like either the most romantic thing that could happen or a setup for serious embarrassment."

"Why embarrassing?" his grandfather asked practically.

"Because I've been more honest in those letters than I've been with anyone in years. I've shared thoughts about what I want from life, what scares me, what makes me feel truly connected to another person." He resumed pacing, his hands moving as he talked. "If Danielle is Maplewood Muse, then she knows I've been thinking about her—about us—in ways I'd never have the courage to say out loud."

"And she's been doing the same thing," his grandmother pointed out with the wisdom of someone who'd watched many love stories unfold. "If your theory is correct, then she's been sharing equally personal thoughts with you. That's not embarrassing, dear—that's beautiful."

"But what if I'm wrong? What if they're two different people and I'm seeing connections that don't exist because I want them to exist?"

"Then you'll figure that out tomorrow evening," his grandfather said practically. "But from what you've told us about both relationships, you're developing genuine feelings either way. Maybe the question isn't whether they're the same person, but whether you're ready to be honest about what you want."

His grandmother nodded in agreement. "Sometimes the heart recognizes what the mind hasn't figured out yet. If this young woman is both your intellectual sparring partner and your thoughtful correspondent, then you've found something rare—someone who challenges you, supports you, and sees you clearly enough to care about both your strengths and your areas for growth."

"That's what makes it so terrifying," Darius admitted, settling back into his chair. "Whether it's one person or two, I care more than I expected to. More than feels safe."

"Love rarely feels safe," his grandmother observed, picking up her knitting again. "If it did, it wouldn't be worth having. The best relationships are the ones that push us to become better versions of ourselves."

"What if she doesn't feel the same way? What if I've been reading too much into the letters, or into our dinner Saturday night?"

"Then you'll know that too," his grandfather said gently. "But Darius, from what I observed Sunday morning when you came by for coffee, you looked happier than you have since you moved back to Sweetgum. Whatever happened on that date, it was good for you."

The memory of Saturday night—Danielle's laughter across the dinner table, the way she'd leaned into their conversations, the softness in her eyes when he'd kissed her goodnight—sent warmth through his chest. "It was good. Really good. She's not who I thought she was when we first met."

"People rarely are," his grandmother said with a smile. "That's what makes getting to know them so interesting."

They talked for another hour, his grandparents sharing stories from their own courtship and early marriage, offering gentle wisdom about navigating uncertainty and taking emotional risks. By the time he walked home through the quiet streets, Darius felt more settled about tomorrow's meeting, whatever it might bring.

Back in his apartment, he reread Maplewood Muse's latest letter, studying her words for clues he might have missed. Her enthusiasm about meeting, her references to shared experiences that seemed to mirror his own, the way she wrote about

Thursday evening with such specific anticipation—everything pointed toward Danielle.

But more than the circumstantial evidence, it was the voice itself that convinced him. The thoughtfulness, the humor, the genuine curiosity about life and literature—it all felt like the woman he'd had dinner with Saturday night, the woman who'd challenged his assumptions and then helped him create something better.

He pulled out his phone and scrolled to Danielle's contact information, thumb hovering over her number. He could call her, ask directly if she was Maplewood Muse, end the uncertainty with a simple conversation. But something held him back—maybe the romantic appeal of letting the mystery unfold naturally, or maybe the fear that being wrong would complicate both relationships.

Instead, he set the phone aside and prepared for bed, trying to calm his racing thoughts. Tomorrow evening would bring answers, one way or another. Whether Maplewood Muse turned out to be Danielle or someone entirely different, he was ready to discover what came next.

As he settled into bed, Darius reflected on how much his life had changed in just a few weeks. The defensive, isolated man who'd been so concerned with protecting literary culture had been replaced by someone willing to take risks on connection, to be vulnerable with people who mattered to him.

Whether that transformation was due to one remarkable woman or two, he was grateful for it. And tomorrow evening, surrounded by the books that had brought them together in the first place, he would finally learn whether the heart could indeed recognize what the mind was still trying to understand.

The anticipation was almost unbearable, but it was also delicious. Because sometimes the best moments in life were the ones that came after waiting, after wondering, after being brave enough to hope for something beautiful.

CHAPTER THIRTEEN

Thursday afternoon dragged by with the slowness of molasses, every interaction feeling like it was keeping Danielle from the evening that might change everything. She'd received Evergreen's response Tuesday morning, and his confirmation of their Thursday evening meeting had sent her pulse into overdrive ever since.

Thursday evening, after the store closes at six.

The specificity had been the final confirmation she needed. Only someone who worked at the bookstore would suggest meeting there after closing hours. Only Darius could make that promise about being there regardless, organizing inventory or reading in the back corner where they kept the comfortable chairs.

Which meant that in approximately two hours, she would finally discover whether her anonymous correspondent and the man who'd been occupying her thoughts since their perfect Saturday night dinner were one and the same.

"You're distracted today," Janet observed, glancing over from her computer screen where she'd been working on the same spreadsheet for the past twenty minutes. "Everything okay? You've been staring at that quarterly report like it contains the secrets of the universe."

"Just have plans tonight that I'm nervous about," Danielle admitted, trying to focus on the numbers that seemed to blur together every time she attempted to concentrate. She'd been working on the same data analysis for three days, and normally she could complete such a report in her sleep.

"Good nervous or bad nervous?"

"I honestly don't know yet." Danielle saved her work and leaned back in her chair, giving up any pretense of productivity. "Have you ever had one of those moments where you're about to find out something that could change everything, but you're not sure if you want the answer?"

Janet's eyebrows rose with interest. "That sounds like either a job interview or a relationship development. Given the way you've been glowing since Monday, I'm guessing relationship."

Heat crept up Danielle's neck. She'd been trying to keep her growing feelings about Darius private, but apparently her emotional state was more transparent than she'd hoped. "Something like that."

"Well, whatever it is, I hope it works out the way you want it to." Janet's smile was genuinely warm. "You deserve something good, Danielle. You've been working so hard lately, and frankly, you've seemed happier this week than you have in months."

At four-thirty, Danielle gave up any pretense of productivity and gathered her things. The October afternoon was crisp and clear, with the kind of golden light that made everything look like it belonged in a romantic movie. She passed the bookstore on her way home and couldn't resist stealing a glance through the windows. Darius was behind the counter, helping an elderly customer select books from a display of local histories. Even from the sidewalk, she could see the patient attention he gave to the woman's questions, the genuine interest he showed in connecting her with exactly what she was looking for.

In her apartment, she stood before her closet paralyzed by indecision. What did one wear to meet an anonymous correspondent who might be the man you'd already started falling for? Something casual felt too dismissive of the moment's significance, but something formal felt presumptuous about outcomes that weren't guaranteed.

She pulled out three different outfits before settling on a knee-length dress in deep green—the same color she'd worn as a sweater to their Saturday dinner, she realized with a flutter of nervous excitement. The dress was casual enough for a book-store meeting but dressy enough to show she'd put thought into the occasion, with three-quarter sleeves that would be comfort-able in the evening air.

As she applied light makeup and ran a brush through her curls, Danielle found herself thinking about all the letters she'd exchanged with Evergreen. The thoughtful questions about finding meaning in work, the observations about literature and connection, the gradual revelation of someone who cared deeply about sharing stories in ways that brought people together rather than keeping them apart.

If her suspicions were correct, then every honest thought she'd shared with her anonymous correspondent had been going to Darius. Every admission about her dreams, her fears, her growing feelings for someone who'd started as an intellec-tual adversary—he'd known it all along.

The thought should have been embarrassing, but instead it filled her with anticipation. If Darius was Evergreen, then their Saturday night dinner had been even more meaningful than she'd realized. All those moments of connection, the feeling that he understood her on a level deeper than casual dating usually allowed—it would all make perfect sense.

At five-thirty, she walked slowly down Main Street toward

the bookstore, her heart hammering with each step. The evening air was cool and crisp, carrying the scent of woodsmoke from someone's fireplace and the faint aroma of dinner preparations drifting from restaurant vents.

She stayed across the street to avoid being spotted too early, watching from a distance as warm light spilled from the book-store windows. She could just make out Darius's silhouette as he moved through what appeared to be his closing routine. He kept glancing toward the windows and checking his watch more than seemed necessary for simply locking up.

When she saw him flip the sign to "Closed" and dim the main lights, leaving only the warm reading lamps glowing in the back corner, she knew it was time. She crossed the street, took a deep breath to steady her nerves, and knocked gently on the door.

The sound of his footsteps approaching made her pulse skip and race. She could hear him pause just inside the door, prob-ably looking through the glass to see who was there. Then the lock turned, and the door opened, and she found herself looking up into dark eyes that widened with recognition, surprise, and something that looked unmistakably like relief.

"Maplewood Muse," he said quietly, and it wasn't a question.

"Evergreen," she replied, her voice barely above a whisper.

For a moment that felt like an eternity, they simply stared at each other. The weight of weeks of anonymous correspondence seemed to hang in the air between them—all the letters, all the careful revelations, all the growing intimacy of shared thoughts that had led to this moment of recognition.

"I had hoped," Darius said finally, stepping back to let her enter the dimly lit store. "But I was afraid to assume."

"The coincidences were getting hard to ignore," Danielle admitted, stepping into the familiar space that looked different somehow in the soft light of evening. The usual bustle of daytime customers was gone, replaced by an intimate quiet that made every sound seem amplified. "Your letters about literature accessibility, the timing of everything, the way you wrote about developing feelings for someone who'd started as an intellectual adversary."

He closed the door behind her and turned the lock, ensuring their privacy for whatever conversation was about to unfold.

"Are you disappointed?" he asked, vulnerability clear in his expression as he turned to face her fully. "That it's me?"

The question caught her off guard with its sincerity. She could see genuine uncertainty in his eyes, as if he truly wasn't sure whether she'd be pleased or dismayed by this revelation.

"Disappointed? Darius, I've been hoping it was you for days. Ever since I started recognizing your voice in those letters." She moved closer, drawn by the warmth in his eyes and the familiar way he was looking at her—the same expression she'd seen during their Saturday dinner, but weighted now with new understanding. "I kept finding parallels between things you'd say and things Evergreen would write, but I was afraid to believe it could be that perfect a coincidence."

Relief flooded his features, and she could see his shoulders relax as tension he'd been carrying for days finally released. "I wasn't sure. We started off on such a combative note, and then the letters were so intimate. I was afraid you might feel like I'd been deceiving you somehow, or that the anonymity was what made our correspondence work."

"You weren't deceiving me. We were both being honest about who we are—just in different contexts." She stepped closer, close enough to catch the familiar scent of his cologne mixed with the comforting smell of books and paper. "If anything, the letters helped me understand why I was so drawn to arguing with you that first day. You challenged me in ways I needed to be challenged."

"And you called me on assumptions I needed to examine." He reached up to brush a curl away from her face, the same gentle gesture from their first date but weighted now with weeks of written intimacy. "God, Danielle. Do you know how many times I've wanted to tell you things I'd only shared with Maplewood Muse?"

"Like what?"

"Like how much I've been looking forward to your letters. Like how you've changed the way I think about literature and connection and what it means to share something you love." His thumb traced along her cheek with infinite gentleness. "Like how I've been falling for you in two different ways and wondering if I was crazy for caring so much about both."

The confession sent warmth spreading through her chest like sunlight breaking through clouds. "You weren't crazy. I've been doing the same thing—looking forward to Evergreen's letters while thinking about our dinner, wondering how someone could make me feel so understood both on paper and in person."

"And now?"

She stepped closer, close enough to see the flecks of gold in his dark eyes, to feel the warmth radiating from his body. "Now I know why both connections felt so right. They were both you."

When he kissed her, it felt like the natural conclusion to weeks of building intimacy—the physical expression of emotional connection they'd been developing through careful words and shared vulnerabilities. His lips were warm and sure against hers, and when she kissed him back, she could feel weeks of anticipation and hope pouring into the moment.

This kiss was different from their Saturday night goodnight kiss, though equally wonderful. That one had been about new discovery, about taking a risk on attraction and possibility. This one was about recognition, about pieces finally falling into place in ways that made perfect sense.

When they finally broke apart, both breathless, Darius rested his forehead against hers.

"I should probably confess something," he said quietly.

"What?"

"I've reread every one of your letters at least three times. Some of them more than that."

She laughed, the sound bright and joyful in the quiet bookstore. "I've done the same thing. I have them memorized at this point. I could probably recite your letter about building bridges instead of barriers word for word."

"So what happens now?" he asked, though his arms around her waist suggested he had some ideas about the answer.

"Now we don't have to choose between Evergreen and Darius, or between Maplewood Muse and Danielle." She smiled up at him, feeling lighter than she had in weeks. "Now we get to be ourselves, completely, with someone who already knows our thoughts and our hearts."

"I like the sound of that," he murmured, and kissed her again.

Outside, the evening light was fading over Main Street, but here in the bookstore, surrounded by stories of every kind, Danielle felt like she'd found exactly where she belonged.

"Thank you," she said softly, her hands resting on his chest where she could feel his heartbeat.

"For what?"

"For being brave enough to suggest we meet. For being exactly who I hoped you'd be." She paused, looking around at the books surrounding them. "For teaching me that the best connections happen when we're willing to be completely honest about who we are."

"Thank you for challenging me to be better," he replied. "Both in person and in letters. You've changed everything about how I see my work, my life, my future."

As they stood there together, Danielle couldn't help but marvel at how perfectly everything had fallen into place. Sometimes, she thought, the best stories really were the ones that surprised you by being exactly what you needed.

CHAPTER FOURTEEN

Danielle woke up Friday morning with a smile she couldn't suppress, her mind immediately drifting to Thursday evening's perfect revelation. The mysterious Evergreen was Darius, the argumentative bookstore owner was her thoughtful correspondent, and somehow both discoveries felt perfectly right rather than shocking.

She lay in bed for a few extra minutes, savoring the memory of standing in the bookstore surrounded by all those stories, finally understanding that the two connections she'd been developing were actually one beautiful, complex relationship. The way Darius had looked at her when she'd knocked on the door, the relief and joy in his voice when he'd said "Maplewood Muse"—it had been like watching puzzle pieces click into place.

Her phone buzzed with a text from him.

Good morning, Maplewood Muse. Still processing last night, but wanted you to know I'm looking forward to our first "official" correspondence now that we know who we're writing to.

The message sent warmth flooding through her chest. Even knowing his identity, he was still thinking about their letters, still wanting to maintain that intimate form of communication that had brought them together.

She typed back.

> Good morning, Evergreen. Last night was perfect. Though I have to admit, part of me will miss the mystery of not knowing who was making me think so deeply about everything.

His response came quickly.

> We can still surprise each other. I don't think knowing faces changes the fact that we're both still figuring out who we are and what we want.

The thoughtfulness of his reply was so quintessentially him—both the letter-writing Evergreen and the in-person Darius who'd gradually revealed himself to be much more complex than his initial defensive facade had suggested.

At work, Danielle found herself unusually productive, the contentment from finally understanding her feelings translating into efficiency with her quarterly analysis. For the first time in weeks, the spreadsheets felt manageable rather than overwhelming. She'd solved the mystery that had been occupying her thoughts, and now she could focus on the equally exciting question of what came next.

Her coworkers seemed to notice the change in her mood. Janet commented on how much lighter she seemed, and even her supervisor Patricia mentioned that her latest reports showed renewed attention to detail.

"You seem happier lately," Janet observed during their coffee break. "Whatever's been going on in your personal life, it's agreeing with you."

"Things are... clarifying," Danielle said carefully, not quite ready to share the full story of anonymous correspondence and romantic revelations. "Sometimes you don't realize how much uncertainty was weighing on you until it's resolved."

When Chrysta called at lunch, Danielle was ready with answers, though she stepped outside to take the call privately.

"So?" her sister demanded without preamble. "Was your pen pal mystery man actually your bookstore guy?"

"He was." Danielle settled onto a bench outside her office building, enjoying the autumn sunshine. "It was Darius all along."

"And how do you feel about that? Because when you first told me about your suspicions, you seemed torn between excitement and terror."

"Like the universe has a sense of humor, but also like everything makes sense now." She paused, trying to find words for the contentment settling in her chest like a warm blanket. "All those letters where he was working through his assumptions about literature and connection—I was watching him do that same work in person. And all my responses about learning to see past first impressions and meeting people where they are—I was living that with him too."

"So you were basically falling for the same person twice without knowing it."

"Exactly. And now I don't have to choose between the thoughtful correspondent and the passionate bookstore owner, because they're the same man." Danielle laughed, still marveling at the coincidence. "I was worried about having feelings for two different people, but it turns out I was just discovering different facets of the same person."

"That's either incredibly romantic or the result of living in a town so small that coincidences like this are inevitable."

Danielle considered this. "Why can't it be both? Maybe small towns create the conditions for these kinds of connections because you can't hide behind anonymity forever. Eventually, you have to reveal who you really are."

"Speaking of revealing who you really are, what happens now? Do you keep writing letters even though you know each other's identities?"

"I think so. There's something special about the way we communicate in writing—more thoughtful, more deliberate. I don't want to lose that just because we know each other's faces."

After they hung up, Danielle found herself looking forward to the end of the workday with an anticipation that felt different from her usual Friday afternoon restlessness. Instead of simply wanting to escape the office, she was eager to see Darius again, to continue navigating this new phase of their relationship.

That evening, she found herself walking toward the bookstore after work, drawn by the prospect of seeing him in his natural habitat with completely new eyes. The late October air was crisp and clear, and the warm light spilling from the store windows made it look especially inviting.

Through the glass, she could see him helping an elderly customer select books from his accessible display, and the sight made her heart warm with affection that felt both familiar and fresh. She could see the patience in his posture, the genuine interest he showed in connecting the woman with exactly what she was looking for—all qualities she'd come to love through their correspondence before she'd recognized them in person.

The bell chimed as she entered, and when he looked up, the smile that spread across his face was worth any slight awkwardness about not knowing exactly how to navigate their new dynamic in public.

"Back again?" he asked, approaching the counter with eyes that held private warmth and something that looked like barely contained delight.

"Thought I'd browse," she said innocently, enjoying the game they seemed to be playing. "Maybe see if you have any good recommendations for someone interested in expanding their literary horizons."

"I might have a few ideas." He came around the counter, standing close enough that she could smell his cologne and catch the warmth radiating from his body. "What kinds of stories speak to you?"

"Oh, you know. Stories about people who start off thinking they understand each other and then discover they were completely wrong." She tilted her head, enjoying the way his eyes sparkled with amusement. "Preferably with some intellectual sparring and unexpected revelations."

"Hmm." He pretended to consider seriously, one hand stroking his chin in exaggerated thoughtfulness. "I think I know exactly what you need."

He led her to the classics section and pulled out a copy of *Passion at Pemberly Manor*—not a pristine edition, but a well-loved paperback with slightly worn edges and what looked like margin notes in faded pencil.

"This one's about a woman who thinks she has a man figured out based on first impressions," he said, holding the book between them with careful reverence. "Turns out she was seeing only the surface."

"And him?"

"He thinks she's beneath his notice at first. Takes him a while to realize she's exactly what he's been looking for."

Danielle accepted the book, noting the way their fingers brushed during the exchange and how the simple touch sent electricity up her arm. "Sounds like they both needed to learn something about assumptions."

"They did. But the story's really about how the best relationships happen when people challenge each other to grow." He paused, his expression growing more serious. "And about how sometimes the people who irritate us most are the ones who see our potential most clearly."

The moment stretched between them, charged with new understanding and the promise of possibilities they were only beginning to explore. The bookstore felt different around them —not just a place of business, but a sanctuary where their story had unfolded through arguments and revelations and finally, recognition.

Then the bell chimed again, and Mrs Andrews entered with her usual purposeful energy, immediately zeroing in on them with the focused attention of someone whose hobby was monitoring local romantic developments.

"Oh my," she said, taking in the scene with obvious delight. "Don't you two look cozy."

Danielle felt heat creep up her neck, but Darius simply smiled with the confidence of someone who'd stopped trying to hide his feelings. "Mrs Andrews. Can we help you find anything?"

"Just picking up the book I ordered. But I couldn't help noticing—" She gestured between them with barely contained excitement. "This looks very promising indeed."

"We're just discussing literature," Danielle said, though she was smiling despite herself.

"Of course you are, dear. That's how all the best romances start—with passionate conversations about books." Mrs Andrews collected her order and headed for the door, pausing to add with maternal authority, "You should bring her to Sunday dinner at your grandparents', Darius. I'm sure they'd love to get to know her better."

After she left, Danielle and Darius looked at each other and burst into laughter.

"Well," he said, "I give it about ten minutes before the entire hit-and-run squad knows we were having an intimate conversation about *Passion at Pemberly Manor*."

"Intimate conversation about literature," Danielle corrected with mock seriousness. "Much more scandalous than regular romance."

"Exactly what this town needs—more intellectual passion," he laughed.

As they talked, other customers filtered in and out, and Danielle found herself helping in small ways that felt natural rather than presumptuous. She directed someone to the cookbook section when Darius was busy with another customer, recommended a mystery series to a teenager who looked overwhelmed by choices, and helped an elderly man find large-print editions of classic westerns.

Working alongside Darius felt like something they'd been doing for years rather than something that had started less than twenty-four hours ago. Their movements around the store were synchronized, their interactions with customers complementary, their shared glances full of private understanding.

"You're good at this," he observed during a quiet moment when the store had emptied of browsers.

"At what?"

"Helping people find what they're looking for. Making them feel welcome." He leaned against the counter, studying her with appreciation. "You should consider spending more time here."

The suggestion sent a flutter through her chest that was part excitement, part nervousness. "Careful. I might take you up on that."

"I'm counting on it," he said quietly, and something in his tone suggested he meant more than just occasional visits.

As closing time approached, Darius began his end-of-day routine while Danielle browsed the poetry section, no longer pretending her visit was purely casual. She pulled out a collection by Mary Oliver, reading the back cover while very aware of him moving around the store, straightening displays and organizing the day's receipts.

When he flipped the sign to "Closed," she felt that same anticipation as the night before—the sense that they were entering private space where they could be completely themselves without the performance of public propriety.

"So," he said, his voice low as he approached silently behind her while she stood reading the back cover of the poetry collection. He slipped his arms around her waist, pulling her back against his chest. She melted into him instantly, her head falling back against his shoulder as his breath warmed her ear. "How does it feel to know your mysterious correspondent's identity?"

"Like I can finally stop analyzing every letter for clues about who you might be," she admitted, her voice breathier than usual as his hands settled lightly on her hips. She turned in his arms, the poetry book forgotten as she looked up into his dark eyes. "Though I have to say, some of your revelations make more sense now. All those comments about learning to share your love of books more generously—I was watching you do exactly that."

"And your insights about meeting people where they are instead of where you think they should be—you were teaching me that in real time." He backed her gently against the bookshelf, his hands braced on either side of her as he leaned closer. "I was falling in love with my teacher without realizing it."

The words sent heat flooding through her, and she reached up to trace the line of his jaw. "I keep thinking about that first day, when I challenged your window display. If I hadn't been so irritated about work, if you hadn't been so defensive about your choices—"

"We might never have had that spark," he finished, catching her hand and pressing a soft kiss to her palm. "Never would have noticed each other enough to end up as pen pals."

"Do you think Mrs Williams knew? When she matched us?" she asked, though her focus was more on the way his thumb was tracing circles on her wrist than on the actual question.

"She's perceptive enough," he murmured, his free hand coming up to cup her face. "And she did say some correspondences seemed to touch something more profound than others. Maybe she saw something we didn't see yet."

"Hearts recognizing hearts, even when minds don't realize it yet."

"Exactly." He leaned his forehead against hers, their bodies pressed together between the poetry shelves. "I'm glad we found each other, Danielle. Both ways."

"Me too." She smiled up at him, her hands fisting in the front of his shirt. "Though I have to warn you—now that I know you're both the man I've been debating literature with and the one whose letters make me think about everything differently, my expectations are pretty high."

"Good," he said, his voice rough with want as he captured her lips in a kiss that was deeper and more urgent than any they'd shared before. "I'd rather aim high and have something worth reaching for."

CHAPTER FIFTEEN

 arius stood behind the counter of Sweetgum Bookstore Saturday morning, trying to concentrate on inventory logs while stealing glances at Danielle, who was curled up in one of the reading chairs with a cup of coffee and the latest issue of *Poetry Magazine*. Having her spend her weekend mornings in the store had become a natural progression of their relationship over the past few weeks, and he found her presence both comforting and distracting in the best possible way.

The morning light streaming through the windows caught the highlights in her dark hair, and every few minutes she'd make a soft sound of appreciation at something she was reading, which made focusing on wholesale orders nearly impossible. She'd arrived with fresh croissants from the bakery down the street and her own coffee, settling into what had apparently become "her" chair without any discussion about whether he minded her claiming space in his store.

He didn't mind. In fact, he was discovering that he liked having someone to share his Saturday morning routine with, someone who understood that quiet companionship could be as intimate as conversation.

"Listen to this," she said suddenly, looking up from her magazine. "This poet writes about finding love letters hidden in library books—apparently someone was using the poetry section as their personal postal service for years before the librarians caught on."

"Romantic or creepy?" Darius asked, setting down his pen to give her his full attention.

"Both? There's something beautiful about the idea of anonymous connection through shared books, but also something invasive about using public property for private correspondence." She paused, a slight smile playing at her lips. "Though I suppose we can't judge too harshly, given our own history with anonymous letter-writing."

The mention of their correspondence sent a familiar warmth through his chest. Even now, weeks after their revelation, the memory of discovering they'd been falling for each other in two different ways still felt miraculous.

The bell chimed, and Mrs Williams entered with a purposeful stride and barely contained excitement that immediately put Darius on alert. The librarian had been practically glowing with satisfaction since their pen-pal identities had been revealed, and her expression suggested she had plans that would somehow involve them.

"Good morning, you two," she said, approaching the counter with a knowing smile that made Danielle look up from her magazine with obvious curiosity. "I hope you don't mind the interruption, but I have some news about the pen-pal program."

Danielle closed her magazine and rose from her chair, moving to stand beside Darius behind the counter in a gesture of unconscious solidarity that didn't go unnoticed by Mrs Williams. They'd been together officially for several weeks now, but the novelty of their unusual origin story still made them both slightly self-conscious whenever it was mentioned in public.

"What kind of news?" Darius asked, though something in Mrs Williams' tone suggested he might not entirely like the answer.

"Well, the program has been such a success that the library board wants to host a community celebration—a reveal event where pen-pal pairs can choose to meet publicly and share their experiences." Mrs Williams's eyes twinkled with mischief as she delivered what was clearly meant to be exciting news. "It would be next Friday evening at the community center, with refreshments and testimonials about the power of written connection."

Darius felt his stomach tighten. While he was grateful for the program that had brought him and Danielle together, the idea of standing in front of the entire community to discuss their correspondence felt uncomfortably exposing. Their letters had been intimate, honest, full of thoughts and feelings he'd never intended to share with anyone beyond their intended recipient.

"That sounds lovely in theory," Danielle said carefully, and he could hear the diplomatic tone she used when trying not to offend someone while expressing reservations. "But wouldn't that violate the anonymity that made the program work in the first place?"

"Only for people who choose to participate," Mrs Williams assured her quickly. "Completely voluntary, of course. Some correspondents have become good friends and are eager to meet publicly, while others prefer to keep their connections private. But I was hoping—" She paused meaningfully, her gaze moving between them. "Well, you two are such a perfect example of how the program can facilitate meaningful connections. Your story could inspire others to be more open to unexpected relationships."

"Our story?" Darius repeated, though he suspected he knew exactly where this was heading.

"Oh, don't pretend you don't know what I'm talking about." Mrs Williams laughed with the indulgent amusement of someone who'd been watching a romance unfold from the beginning. "The whole town has been observing your courtship—first the literary debates, then the community service collaboration, now the obvious romance blossoming in full view of anyone who walks past this store. Adding the pen-pal element just makes it even more charming."

Heat crept up Darius's neck as he realized that their relationship had apparently been community entertainment from the very beginning. "Mrs Williams, I'm not sure we're comfortable being the poster couple for—"

"Just think about it," she interrupted gently, her expression shifting to something more maternal and persuasive. "No pressure, but your story could help other people believe in the possibility of finding real connection, both through letters and in person. In a world where everyone seems to communicate through screens, you've proven that thoughtful correspondence can still lead to lasting relationships."

The request hung in the air between them as Mrs Williams gathered her things and headed toward the door with the satisfied expression of someone who'd planted a seed and was confident it would grow in the right direction.

After she left, the store fell into uncomfortable silence. Darius returned to his inventory logs, but the numbers seemed to blur together as he became hyperaware of Danielle's presence and the weight of Mrs Williams's request. He could feel tension radiating from her, though she'd returned to her chair and was making a show of reading her magazine.

"So," Danielle said finally, her voice carefully neutral, "thoughts on being the featured love story at a community event?"

"Honestly? The idea terrifies me." Darius set down his pen and looked at her directly, abandoning any pretense of working.

"Our letters were private. Personal. The thought of discussing them in front of people we barely know feels..."

"Invasive," she finished, and he could hear relief in her voice that he understood her discomfort. "I agree. Though I have to admit, part of me is flattered that Mrs Williams thinks our connection is worth celebrating."

"It is worth celebrating," he said quietly. "But maybe not in front of an audience of people who've apparently been watching us like we're characters in their favorite television show."

The revelation that their entire relationship had been under community observation was more unsettling than he'd expected. He'd known that small towns had limited privacy, but the idea that their arguments, their growing connection, even their quiet moments together had been noted and discussed felt suffocating.

The bell chimed again, and Darius looked up to see the hit-and-run squad entering en masse—Mrs Andrews, Mrs Bridges, and Mrs Craskin, all wearing expressions of barely contained excitement that suggested they'd already heard about Mrs Williams's proposal.

"We heard about the pen-pal reveal event," Mrs Andrews announced without preamble, approaching the counter with the determination of someone on a mission. "How exciting that you two will be the featured couple!"

"We haven't agreed to anything," Darius said quickly, feeling cornered by the assumption that their participation was a foregone conclusion.

"Oh, but you must," Mrs Bridges insisted, her voice carrying the tone of someone who couldn't imagine why anyone would hesitate to share their personal life with the entire community. "Your story is so romantic—the enemies-to-lovers arc, the secret correspondence, the dramatic revelation. It's like something out of a novel."

"Our lives aren't entertainment," Danielle said with more

edge than usual, and Darius could see her shoulders tensing as she spoke.

Mrs Craskin looked taken aback by the sharpness in Danielle's voice. "Of course not, dear. We just think it's beautiful how you found each other. In a town this size, genuine love stories are worth celebrating and sharing with others who might be losing hope about finding connection themselves."

"We appreciate that," Darius said diplomatically, "but we need some time to think about it."

"Don't think too long," Mrs Andrews advised as the trio prepared to leave. "Mrs Williams will need to finalize the program soon, and everyone's so excited to hear how your correspondence began."

After they left, Darius noticed Danielle's tension in the set of her shoulders, the way she'd closed her magazine without marking her place and was now staring out the window with a troubled expression.

"You okay?" he asked, coming around the counter to sit in the chair beside hers.

"I don't like feeling like we're on display," she admitted, turning to face him with vulnerability that made his chest tight. "Like our relationship exists for other people's entertainment or inspiration. When did our private correspondence become public property?"

"Me neither." The pressure was more intense than he'd anticipated, and he was beginning to understand why some people chose to keep their relationships completely private. "Though I have to ask—are you having second thoughts about us? About how public this has all become?"

"About us? No." Her response was immediate and firm, which sent relief flooding through him. "About living in a fish-bowl where every conversation becomes community gossip and every gesture gets analyzed for romantic significance? Maybe."

The honesty stung, even though he understood her frustration. The constant attention from well-meaning neighbors was beginning to feel suffocating, especially when it came to pressure about sharing their private correspondence with people who had no right to those intimate details.

"We could say no to the event," he offered. "Tell Mrs Williams we appreciate the invitation but prefer to keep our story private."

"And deal with weeks of disappointed looks and gentle persuasion from everyone who thinks we're being unnecessarily secretive?" She ran a hand through her curls, a gesture he'd learned meant she was working through complicated feelings. "In a town like this, refusing to participate in community celebrations is seen as antisocial rather than simply private."

She had a point that made him uncomfortable. Sweetgum's culture of community involvement was one of the things he'd appreciated about moving back, but he was learning that it came with expectations about sharing personal milestones and allowing neighbors to feel invested in your private business.

The rest of the day passed with underlying tension neither of them seemed able to shake. Customers continued to comment on their "sweet romance" and make jokes about "lovebirds" and "the bookstore's happy ending." Each comment felt like another small violation of privacy, another reminder that their relationship was considered public entertainment.

Mrs Patterson mentioned how romantic it was that they'd found love through letters. The teenager browsing graphic novels asked if they were planning to write a book about their experience. Even delivery drivers seemed to have heard about the "bookstore love story" and offered congratulations that made Darius want to hide in his storage room. Darius was an introvert at heart and this felt like an introvert's nightmare. He suspected Danielle felt the same.

By evening, when they walked to Rochelle's for dinner, Danielle was quieter than usual, lost in thought in a way that made him increasingly anxious about what conclusions she might be reaching.

"You're thinking," he observed as they paused at a crosswalk.

"I'm always thinking."

"You're thinking something specific. Something that's bothering you."

She stopped walking and turned to face him under a streetlight, her expression serious in a way that made his stomach clench with apprehension. "I love what we have, Darius. I love that we found each other through letters, love that we can debate literature and challenge each other and be completely ourselves together."

"But?" The word came out more sharply than he'd intended, braced as he was for whatever reservation was coming.

"But I'm starting to feel like we're not allowed to just be a couple. Like we have to be the town's romantic success story, proof that love can happen in unexpected ways." She ran both hands through her curls in frustration. "I didn't sign up to be anyone's inspiration or to have my private letters become community property."

Darius felt something cold settle in his stomach. "Are you saying you want to step back? Take a break from being so visible?"

"I'm saying I want to be able to have a relationship without commentary from three different busybodies every time we're seen together." Her voice carried frustration he'd never heard before, edged with exhaustion from constant scrutiny. "I want to be able to figure out what we are without pressure to be what everyone else thinks we should be."

The words hit him harder than he'd expected. He'd been so grateful for their connection, so pleased by the community's approval and investment in their happiness, that he hadn't considered how the constant attention might be affecting her differently than it affected him.

"So what do you want to do?"

"I don't know," she said quietly, and the uncertainty in her voice was almost worse than anger would have been. "But I think we need to talk about whether this—" She gestured between them, then around at the town surrounding them. "Whether this is what we both actually want, or if we're just caught up in everyone else's expectations about our story."

As they continued toward the restaurant, Darius found himself questioning everything he'd been taking for granted about their relationship. Was their connection as strong as he'd believed, or had they been influenced by community pressure and romantic circumstances beyond their actual compatibility?

The uncertainty felt like standing on shifting ground, and for the first time since discovering Danielle was Maplewood Muse, he wondered if finding each other had been as perfect as it had seemed, or if they were about to discover that real love required more than romantic coincidences and community approval.

CHAPTER SIXTEEN

anielle sat in her apartment Sunday evening, staring at a half-written letter to Evergreen that she'd started and abandoned three times. After their tense conversation the night before, she and Darius had agreed to take a few days to think about what they wanted, separate from community expectations and the pressure of being Sweetgum's featured romance.

The problem was, the more she thought about it, the more confused she became.

She'd spent the day trying to sort through her feelings, alternating between cleaning her apartment with nervous energy and sitting in her reading chair staring out at the street below. The autumn afternoon had been crisp and clear, with families walking past her building on their way to the park, couples holding hands as they window-shopped downtown, ordinary people living ordinary lives without the weight of community investment in their romantic success.

When had her relationship with Darius become so complicated? When had the simple joy of discovering they were each other's anonymous correspondents been overshadowed by expectations and pressure to perform their love story for public consumption?

Her phone buzzed with a text from Aleeyah.

> How are things with bookstore guy? Haven't heard from you in a while.

Danielle stared at the message, unsure how to respond. How could she explain that she was questioning a relationship that had felt perfect just a week ago, simply because other people were too invested in their love story? How could she admit that the very thing that had brought them together—their ability to communicate honestly and deeply—was being threatened by the fishbowl existence of small-town life?

She typed back.

> Complicated. Will call you tomorrow.

The response came immediately.

> Uh oh. What happened?

Instead of answering, Danielle set her phone aside and returned to the letter she'd been struggling to write. Part of her wanted to pour out her confusion to Evergreen, the way she had when their correspondence was truly anonymous and she could be completely honest without worrying about how her words might affect their in-person relationship. But writing to Darius about her doubts regarding their relationship felt strange and circular, like trying to solve a problem by talking to the problem itself.

She'd written three different versions already. The first had been full of questions and uncertainty, asking whether they were real or just caught up in romantic circumstances. The second had been defensive, trying to justify her need for space and privacy. The third had been apologetic, attempting to explain her feelings without hurting his.

None of them felt right. None of them captured what she actually wanted to say, which was that she missed the simplicity of their early connection, before it became performance art for the entertainment of neighbors who meant well but didn't understand the weight of constant observation.

A knock at her door interrupted her spiraling thoughts. She opened it to find Chrysta standing in the hallway with a bottle of wine and a determined expression that suggested she'd been dispatched on a mission of sisterly intervention.

"Aleeyah called me," Chrysta announced, pushing past Danielle into the apartment with the confidence of someone who'd appointed herself family crisis manager. "Said you sounded weird about the bookstore romance and she was worried. Also, you look terrible."

"Thanks for the honesty," Danielle said dryly, though she was grateful for the company. "And I'm fine."

"No, you're not. You're overthinking something, and given that you've been floating on air for weeks talking about Darius, I'm guessing it's relationship-related." Chrysta settled on the couch and opened the wine with practiced efficiency. "Talk to me."

Danielle accepted the glass her sister offered and curled up in the armchair across from her, trying to find words for the tangle of emotions she'd been wrestling with all day. "Have you ever had something good that everyone else was so excited about that you started questioning whether it was actually good, or if you just thought it was good because everyone told you it should be?"

"That's a very philosophical way of avoiding my question," Chrysta observed. "But yes. Remember when I got that promotion to senior analyst and everyone kept telling me how lucky I was?"

"The one where you'd be managing people instead of doing the actual analytical work you loved?"

"Exactly. Suddenly everyone was so excited for me—Mom, Dad, all my colleagues—that I felt guilty for having doubts. I started questioning whether I was being ungrateful or if my instincts about it being wrong for me were actually valid."

Danielle leaned forward with interest. "What did you do?"

"Turned it down and stayed in my current role. Best decision I ever made, even though everyone thought I was crazy." Chrysta took a sip of wine, her expression thoughtful. "Sometimes other people's excitement about your life can drown out your own inner voice. The trick is learning to trust yourself even when everyone else thinks they know what's best for you."

The parallel made Danielle's stomach clench. "So you think I should break up with Darius?"

"I think you should tell me what's actually going on instead of speaking in hypotheticals."

Over the next hour, Danielle found herself explaining everything—the pressure from Mrs Williams and the hit-and-run squad, the uncomfortable feeling of being watched and commented on, the expectation that they'd share their private correspondence for community entertainment, her growing uncertainty about whether her feelings for Darius were genuine or influenced by external expectations.

"The worst part," she concluded, "is that I can't tell anymore what's real and what's performance. When I'm with him, do I feel happy because I actually enjoy his company, or because everyone's watching us and expecting me to be happy? When he kisses me, am I responding to him or to the romantic story everyone thinks we're living?"

"So let me get this straight," Chrysta said when she finished. "You're questioning a relationship with someone who makes you laugh, challenges you intellectually, shares your values, and communicates beautifully in writing—because other people are happy about it?"

"It's not that simple."

"Isn't it?" Chrysta leaned forward, her expression both sympathetic and exasperated. "Danielle, you've been floating on air for weeks. Every time you mention Darius, your whole face lights up. You light up talking about his letters, his sense of humor, the way he's changed his approach to the bookstore. But now you're second-guessing everything because Mrs Andrews makes comments at the grocery store?"

"It's not just comments. It's the constant attention, the expectation that we'll perform our relationship for community entertainment, the pressure to be some kind of romantic ideal—"

"So don't be," Chrysta interrupted. "Be a regular couple who happens to live in a small town where people care about each other's happiness."

Danielle stared at her sister, feeling like she was missing something obvious. "What do you mean?"

"I mean stop letting other people's investment in your story dictate how you feel about the story itself." Chrysta poured herself more wine, settling back into the couch cushions. "You found someone amazing in an unusual way. That's worth celebrating, not hiding from."

"But what if the circumstances made us think we had more in common than we actually do? What if we were just caught up in the romance of anonymous letters and dramatic revelations?"

"Then you'll figure that out by spending time together, not by analyzing your feelings to death." Chrysta gave her a pointed look. "When's the last time you actually talked to him about something other than community pressure and relationship anxiety?"

The question caught Danielle off guard. When had she last asked Darius about his writing, his thoughts on a book he'd read, his dreams for the future? When had they last had the kind of deep, meandering conversation that had drawn her to his letters in the first place?

"I think," she said slowly, the realization hitting her like cold water, "I've been so worried about whether our connection was real that I stopped nurturing the connection itself."

"Bingo." Chrysta smiled with the satisfaction of someone who'd successfully guided another person to an important insight. "So maybe instead of taking a break to 'figure things out,' you should take a break from worrying about what everyone else thinks and focus on what you two actually have together."

"But how do I do that when we can't go anywhere without someone commenting on our 'sweet romance' or asking about wedding plans?"

"You set boundaries. You tell people politely but firmly that your relationship is private. You decline to participate in events that make you uncomfortable. You remember that other people's opinions about your love life are ultimately irrelevant to your actual happiness."

Chrysta reached over and squeezed Danielle's hand. "Look, I get it. Small-town life can feel suffocating when everyone thinks they have a stake in your personal business. But don't let their nosiness rob you of something good. From everything you've told me about Darius, he sounds like someone worth fighting for."

"Even if it means disappointing people who are excited about our story?"

"Especially then. Your job is to live your life, not to be inspiring to other people."

After Chrysta left, Danielle returned to her abandoned letter with new clarity. Instead of analyzing her feelings or questioning their relationship, she found herself writing about the poetry collection she'd been reading, a funny observation about her coworkers, a memory from childhood that had surfaced while walking through downtown that morning.

Dear Evergreen,

I've been thinking about how easy it is to lose sight of what matters when we're too focused on how things appear from the outside. This week I found myself questioning beautiful things simply because other people noticed they were beautiful—as if external validation somehow diminished their authenticity.

But tonight I remembered something important: the reason I fell for your letters wasn't because they were part of a romantic story, but because they showed me someone who thought deeply about life, who cared about books and growth. The reason I enjoyed our early arguments wasn't because they led to romance, but because you challenged me to examine my own assumptions.

I think I got distracted by the fairy-tale aspects of our story and forgot to appreciate the daily reality of knowing someone who makes me think, who makes me laugh, who shares my belief that words matter and human connection is worth working for.

So I wanted to write to you the way I did in the beginning—not as part of any grand romantic narrative, but simply as someone who values your thoughts and wants to share her own.

What's been on your mind lately, beyond all the noise about pen-pal programs and community expectations? What are you reading? What questions are you pondering? What makes you smile when no one's watching?

I miss those conversations, the ones that exist just for us.

Yours truly,
Maplewood Muse

As she sealed the envelope, Danielle felt lighter than she had in days. Whether she and Darius had a future together or not, she wanted to find out based on who they actually were, not who the town thought they should be.

And maybe, just maybe, returning to the kind of honest communication that had brought them together in the first place would help them remember why they'd wanted to be together at all.

The letter felt like a beginning rather than an ending—the start of choosing their relationship over other people's expectations, their authentic connection over the performance of romance.

Monday morning, she would deliver it to the library with anticipation rather than anxiety, curious to see if Darius was ready to rediscover what they'd found in those first anonymous exchanges.

Because sometimes the best way forward was to remember what had worked in the beginning, before the rest of the world had gotten involved in their love story.

CHAPTER SEVENTEEN

Darius read Maplewood Muse's letter three times Monday evening, sitting in his apartment with a cup of coffee growing cold beside him. Her words felt like a lifeline thrown to someone drowning in confusion—a reminder of why he'd been drawn to her correspondence in the first place.

The letter lay open on his small kitchen table, her familiar handwriting bringing back memories of those early weeks when each envelope had been a treasure to anticipate. She'd written about missing their conversations, about getting distracted by fairy-tale narratives when the daily reality of connection was what actually mattered. Reading her words, he realized how much he'd missed this—not just her thoughts, but the way she expressed them with such clarity and honesty.

She was right. They'd gotten so caught up in the romantic narrative of their unusual beginning that they'd stopped nurturing the actual relationship. The deep conversations, the intellectual challenges, the simple pleasure of sharing thoughts with someone who understood—all of that had been buried under community expectations and performance anxiety.

He'd spent the weekend in his own spiral of doubt, questioning whether their connection was real or manufactured, whether he was falling for Danielle herself or for the idea of their story. But reading her letter, he realized he'd been asking the wrong questions entirely. Instead of wondering whether their feelings were "real," he should have been asking whether they wanted to keep building something together.

And the answer to that question was unequivocally yes.

He pulled out paper and began writing, feeling more settled than he had since Mrs Williams had announced the reveal event. The familiar rhythm of composing thoughts for Maplewood Muse felt like coming home to himself.

Dear Maplewood Muse,

Your letter was exactly what I needed to read. I've been so focused on whether we were "real" or just caught up in circumstances that I forgot to pay attention to what made us work in the first place.

You ask what's been on my mind beyond all the noise. Honestly? I've been reading Mary Oliver's poetry collection—the one you were browsing Saturday morning—and thinking about her line: "Tell me, what is it you plan to do with your one wild and precious life?" It makes me wonder if I've been so worried about making the right choices that I've forgotten to make brave ones.

I've also been thinking about the future of the bookstore, about ways to make it more of a community gathering place without losing its essential character. There's something appealing about hosting poetry readings, book clubs for different age groups, maybe even writing workshops.

What makes me smile when no one's watching? This morning I found a note someone had left in a used book —just a simple "this story changed my life, I hope it changes yours too." That kind of quiet generosity, the way books link strangers across time and space.

I miss our conversations too. The ones where we could explore ideas without worrying about outcomes, where disagreement led to understanding rather than argument.

Maybe we could meet—not as part of any community story, but just as two people who enjoy each other's company and want to see where honest conversation leads.

Yours in appreciation of wild and precious lives, Evergreen

As he sealed the letter, Darius felt a sense of rightness he hadn't experienced in days. This was who they were—two people who'd found each other through words and wanted to keep finding each other, regardless of external pressure or expectations.

The next morning, he delivered the letter to Chris Williams at the library, making sure it would reach Maplewood Muse that day. Then he spent the morning reorganizing the bookstore's back corner, creating a more comfortable seating area with better lighting and a small table perfect for two people sharing coffee and conversation.

He'd been thinking about the space differently lately, influenced by Danielle's original criticism about accessibility and his own growing understanding of what the bookstore could become. Instead of a shrine to literary culture that people had to prove themselves worthy of entering, it could be a place where literature lived and breathed and connected people to each other.

The changes were small but significant—moving the chairs closer together, adding a side table for coffee cups and note-books, positioning a small lamp to create warmer lighting. He was creating an invitation to linger, to talk, to treat books as starting points for conversation rather than endpoints in themselves.

Around eleven, the bell chimed and Danielle entered, looking less tense than she had over the weekend. Her shoulders weren't hunched with defensive anxiety, and when she caught sight of him behind the counter, her smile was genuine rather than cautious.

"Hi," she said simply.

"Hi." He came around the counter, noting how natural it felt to move toward her, how much he'd missed even this simple ritual of greeting. "How are you feeling?"

"Better. Clearer." She glanced around the store, taking in the changes he'd made to the reading area with obvious interest. "New setup?"

"I thought it might be nice to have a space designed for actual conversation rather than just browsing." He gestured toward the comfortable chairs and small table he'd arranged. "A place where people could sit together and really talk about what they're reading."

"I think it looks like somewhere two people could get to know each other without an audience."

The comment carried warmth that had been missing from their recent interactions, and he felt some of the tension he'd been carrying in his chest finally begin to ease.

"Would you like to test it out? I made coffee."

"I'd love that."

For the next hour, they sat in the newly arranged space and talked—really talked—for the first time since the community pressure had started building. No discussion of relationship status or external expectations, just genuine conversation about books they'd been reading, ideas they'd been considering, small observations about daily life that felt significant when shared with someone who truly listened.

Danielle told him about a data analysis project that had revealed unexpected patterns in local library usage, and how the discovery had made her think about the hidden stories in everyday life. He shared his thoughts about the Mary Oliver poetry collection, about how her observations of the natural world had made him more aware of the small miracles happening around him daily.

They talked about childhood favorites—how she'd discovered poetry through a teacher who'd read Maya Angelou aloud, how he'd fallen in love with historical fiction after finding a box of his grandfather's war novels in the attic. They debated the merits of different coffee brewing methods, discussed the upcoming local election, shared funny stories about customer interactions and coworker quirks.

"I forgot how much I enjoy this," Danielle said, curled up in her chair with her coffee cup warming her hands.

"Just talking?"

"Talking with you. The way you listen, how you make connections between ideas I wouldn't have thought to link." She paused, studying his face with an expression that was both thoughtful and affectionate. "I think I got so worried about whether we were 'real' that I stopped appreciating what we actually have."

"Me too." Darius leaned forward slightly, drawn by the openness in her expression. "I kept questioning whether our feelings were authentic or just the result of romantic circumstances, but I was asking the wrong question."

"What's the right question?"

"Whether we want to keep getting to know each other,

regardless of how it started." He met her eyes directly, feeling more certain than he had in days. "And I do, Danielle. I want to know what you think about when you're walking to work, what books you loved as a kid, what makes you laugh until you can't breathe. I want to hear your opinions about everything from local politics to the best way to make coffee."

"Even if some of those opinions turn out to be arguments?"

"Especially then. You challenge me in ways that make me better, that make me think more clearly about things I've always taken for granted."

The smile that spread across her face was the first completely unguarded one he'd seen from her in days. "I want that too. All of it."

"And maybe we could meet regularly—not as part of any community story or romantic narrative, but just as two people who enjoy each other's company."

"I'd like that. I like the idea of having our own rhythm, separate from everyone else's expectations."

They were interrupted by the bell chiming and Mrs Patterson entering with her walker, moving slowly but determinedly toward the romance section. As Darius helped her navigate to her usual browsing area, Danielle naturally fell into conversation with the elderly woman about her favorite authors.

"Have you read any LaVyrle Spencer?" Mrs Patterson asked Danielle with the enthusiasm of someone eager to share a literary discovery.

"I haven't, but I should. What do you recommend?"

"Oh, dear, start with *Morning Glory*. It's about a woman who finds love in the most unexpected circumstances, and the writing is just beautiful."

Watching them interact—Danielle's genuine interest, Mrs Patterson's obvious delight in having someone new to discuss books with—Darius felt a contentment that had nothing to do with grand romantic gestures and everything to do with daily compatibility. This was what he wanted: someone who could move seamlessly into his world, who treated his customers with respect and interest, who understood that books were bridges between people rather than barriers.

After Mrs Patterson left with her selections, they returned to their conversation with renewed ease. The afternoon passed quickly, punctuated by other customers but always returning to the comfortable rhythm of two people genuinely interested in each other's thoughts.

A teenage girl browsed the young adult section, and Danielle quietly recommended a fantasy series that had strong female characters. An older man looking for a gift for his wife ended up in a fascinating conversation with both of them about the difference between literary fiction and commercial fiction, leaving with a book none of them had expected him to choose.

"I like this," Danielle said during a quiet moment between customers. "The way we work together, how natural it feels."

"You're good at this. At helping people find what they're looking for."

"Maybe because I know what it's like to be looking for something and not quite know how to ask for it."

The comment carried layers of meaning that made him want to ask deeper questions, but before he could respond, another customer entered and the moment shifted.

"I should probably head home," Danielle said eventually, though she made no move to leave her chair.

"Probably." Darius didn't want the afternoon to end either.

"But maybe I could come by tomorrow? Continue this conversation?"

"I'd like that. I'd like that a lot."

As she gathered her things, Danielle paused by the door. "Darius? Thank you for being patient with me while I figured out what I was worried about."

"Thank you for being honest about what you needed. And for writing that letter—it helped me understand what I was worried about too."

"See you tomorrow?"

"Absolutely."

After she left, Darius looked around the bookstore with new eyes. The reading area he'd created, the comfortable mixing of old and new in his displays, the sense of possibility that came from knowing someone appreciated both his work and his thoughts—it all felt like pieces of a life worth building.

And if that life included someone who challenged him intellectually, supported his dreams, and could debate literature with equal parts passion and humor, then he was ready to stop worrying about the story they were supposed to be telling and start living the one they wanted to write.

Because the best love stories, he was learning, were the ones where two people chose each other daily, not just in grand moments but in quiet conversations and shared laughter and the simple pleasure of being truly known by another person who saw you clearly and wanted to keep looking.

CHAPTER EIGHTEEN

Darius stood in front of his bathroom mirror, adjusting his collar for the third time while trying to calm the nervous energy that had been building all afternoon. Tonight was different. Tonight, he and Danielle were going to stop hiding from the community attention and simply be themselves—a couple in love who refused to let other people's expectations dictate how they lived their lives.

The decision had been brewing since their conversation the week before about Mrs Williams' pen-pal reveal event. Instead of continuing to feel suffocated by the fishbowl existence of small-town romance, they'd chosen to reclaim their story. Starting with dinner at Rochelle's diner, right in the heart of downtown where everyone could see them.

A knock at his apartment door interrupted his preparations. When he opened it, Danielle stood there wearing a deep red dress that brought out her complexion and a smile that suggested she was feeling just as rebellious as he was.

"Ready to scandalize Sweetgum with our public display of affection?" she asked, rising on her toes to kiss him hello.

"With you looking like that, I'm ready to take on the whole town," he replied, his voice warm with affection. The dress was simple but elegant, and the confidence in her posture made his heart skip.

"Good, because I have plans for you tonight, Darius Jones." Her eyes sparkled with mischief as she smoothed her hands over his chest, straightening his collar with unnecessary attention to detail.

"What kind of plans?" he asked.

"The kind that involve reminding you why we stopped caring what other people think."

The drive to Rochelle's diner was filled with comfortable conversation and the easy intimacy that had developed between them over months of growing closer. When his hand found her knee at red lights, when she traced patterns on his forearm while he drove, it felt natural.

Rochelle's diner was exactly what they'd expected—busy with the usual Friday night crowd, warm with the smell of comfort food and the sound of local conversation. As they entered, Darius was aware of the glances that followed them, but instead of the anxiety he'd felt before, he found himself simply not caring. Let people look. He was proud to be with Danielle.

They were seated at a corner booth that offered both intimacy and a view of the room. As they settled across from each other, Darius couldn't help but appreciate how the soft lighting caught the highlights in her dark hair, how her eyes seemed to glow with contentment.

"This is nice," Danielle said, reaching across the table to intertwine their fingers.

"The diner?"

"Being here with you. Not hiding, not worrying about what anyone thinks." She squeezed his hand gently. "Just being us."

"I like being us," he said, bringing her hand to his lips to press a soft kiss to her knuckles. "I like being us a lot."

"Well, look at you two," Aimee said with genuine warmth as she came over and poured their water. "You both look happy tonight."

"We are," Danielle replied, her thumb tracing gentle circles on Darius's hand. "Very happy."

As they ordered and settled into their meal, they fell into the easy rhythm of conversation that had always characterized their relationship. But tonight felt different—more relaxed, more openly affectionate. When Darius reached across to steal a bite of her appetizer, she fed it to him with a laugh. When she told a story about her workday, he found himself watching the animated way she gestured, completely captivated by her enthusiasm.

"I have a confession," she said during a lull in conversation, her voice soft and private despite their public setting.

"Tell me," he encouraged.

"I've been thinking about us," she said

"Good thoughts, I hope," he teased.

"The best thoughts." Her smile was soft and private. "I've been thinking about how much I've come to care about you, about how right this feels." She paused, a sheepish smile on her face. "I keep thinking about how natural it's become, having you in my life this way. I love the way you make everything feel significant, even ordinary moments like sharing coffee or reading together."

The simple honesty in her words made his chest warm with affection. "You do the same for me. You make me notice things I used to take for granted."

Before she could respond, Aimee returned with their entrees. But instead of simply serving their food, she hesitated beside their table with an expression that suggested she had something to say.

"I hope you don't mind me mentioning this," she began carefully, "but I heard through the grapevine that all the attention you've been getting has been making you both uncomfortable."

Darius felt Danielle's hand tighten slightly in his, and he squeezed back reassuringly.

"I just wanted you to know," Aimee continued, her voice gentle but sincere, "when people talk about you two around here, it's never gossip or nosiness. It's genuine happiness. This town has watched both of you—Darius, we've all seen how much you care about that bookstore and bringing literature to people. And Danielle, honey, we've watched you work so hard and be so dedicated to everything you do."

She paused, seeming to gather her thoughts.

"Seeing you find each other, seeing how happy you make each other—it gives people hope. In a world where everything feels uncertain, watching two good people fall in love reminds us that beautiful things still happen. Nobody wants to put pressure on you or make you uncomfortable. We're just genuinely happy for you."

The words hung in the air between them, and Darius felt something shift in his chest. The community attention that had felt suffocating suddenly seemed reframed as something much more generous and genuine.

"Thank you," Danielle said softly, her voice thick with emotion. "That... that means more than you know."

"You're good people," Aimee said simply. "And good people deserve good things. Enjoy your dinner."

After she left, they sat in comfortable silence for a moment, processing her words.

"I feel like we've been looking at this all wrong," Danielle said finally.

"How so?"

"I've been so focused on feeling invaded that I didn't consider the possibility that people were just... happy for us."

She met his eyes across the table. "She's right, isn't she? About the hope thing?"

Darius considered this, thinking about Mrs Patterson's obvious delight in their romance, about the way his grandmother's face lit up whenever she mentioned their relationship, about the genuine warmth in people's congratulations.

"I think she is," he said slowly. "I think we've been seeing attention and assuming it was pressure, when maybe it was just... love. Community love."

"Mrs Williams' pen-pal reveal event," Danielle said quietly.

"What about it?"

"Maybe we should participate. Not because we feel pressured to, but because..." She paused, searching for words. "Because our story might actually help people believe in possibility."

The suggestion sent a flutter of anticipation through his chest, though not for the reasons she might expect. He'd been thinking about the event differently lately, seeing it as a potential opportunity for something much more personal and significant.

"You want to tell our story publicly?"

"I want to honor what brought us together. And if sharing how we found each other through anonymous letters and heated arguments helps even one person believe in love again..." She shrugged, but her expression was thoughtful. "Maybe that's worth stepping into the spotlight."

Darius felt a smile tugging at his lips. "Mrs Williams is going to be beside herself with joy."

"Probably. But that's not why I want to do it."

"Why do you want to do it?"

Danielle was quiet for a moment, absently tracing patterns on the condensation on her water glass. "Because I'm proud of us. I'm proud of what we've built, how we found each other, how we've grown together. And maybe it's time to stop hiding from that pride."

The words sent warmth flooding through his chest. "I'm proud of us too."

"So we'll do it? We'll participate in the reveal event?"

"We'll do it," he confirmed, though his mind was already racing with possibilities he couldn't share with her yet. The event could be perfect timing for what he'd been planning.

The rest of dinner passed in renewed contentment and shared excitement about their decision. They talked about what they might say, how they wanted to frame their story, what it meant to them to honor the program that had brought them together.

When Danielle reached across the table to brush a crumb from his cheek, letting her fingers linger against his skin, he caught her hand and pressed a gentle kiss to her palm.

"What was that for?" she asked softly.

"Just appreciating you. The way you think, the way you see the world, the way you make everything better just by being part of it." He paused, his heart hammering as he looked into her eyes. "I love you, Danielle."

The words hung in the air between them, and he watched as her breath caught, as tears gathered in her eyes, as a smile spread across her face that was more radiant than anything he'd ever seen.

"I love you too," she whispered, her voice thick with emotion. "I've been wanting to say it for weeks, but I was terrified it was too soon."

"It's not too soon," he said, bringing her hand to his lips again. "It's exactly the right time."

As they prepared to leave, Darius felt a deep satisfaction about the evening. They'd made an important decision together, overcome their fears about community attention, and grown closer in the process. But more than that, they'd proven to themselves that they could face anything as long as they faced it together.

"Ready to head back?" he asked as he helped her with her jacket.

"More than ready," she replied, slipping her arm through his as they walked toward the door.

CHAPTER NINETEEN

The drive back to Darius's apartment was quiet, but every mile hummed with the newness of what they'd said at dinner. Their first I love you hovered in the small space like a breath neither of them wanted to release. Even the brush of his knuckles on the gearshift felt charged, significant enough to make Danielle's pulse stumble and then race.

"I can't stop thinking about what you said," she admitted as they climbed the stairs. "About loving me."

"I can't stop thinking about the way you looked when you said it back," he replied, fumbling slightly with his keys. "Like you'd been holding your breath and could finally exhale."

"I had been. For weeks." She touched his forearm, a light press that stilled him. He looked up. "I was afraid it was too soon—that I'd say it out loud and startle everything good between us."

"Nothing about you could scare me off, Danielle." He cupped her face with his free hand, thumb tracing the arc of her cheekbone in a way that felt both reverent and familiar. "You're exactly what I've been looking for my entire life, even when I didn't know I was looking."

When he finally managed to unlock the door, they moved into his small apartment with a new awareness of each other. The space felt different somehow—more intimate, more theirs now that they'd crossed the threshold of spoken love.

"Wine?" he asked, though his voice was slightly rough with something that had nothing to do with thirst.

"Please."

She settled onto his couch while he moved around the small kitchen, but her attention was entirely focused on him—the way his shirt stretched across his shoulders as he reached for glasses, the careful attention he paid to opening the bottle, the slight tremor in his hands that suggested he was as affected by the evening as she was.

When he joined her on the couch, handing her a glass of red wine, she noticed he sat closer than usual. Close enough that she could smell his cologne, could see the gold flecks in his eyes in the soft lamplight.

"To us," he said, raising his glass.

"To finally being brave enough to say what we feel," she replied, clinking her glass against his.

The wine was smooth , a soft warmth blooming in her chest, but it was nothing compared to the heat that spread through her when Darius set his glass down and turned to face her more fully.

"Can I ask you something?" he said, his voice softer than usual.

"Always."

"What changed your mind tonight? About the community attention, about participating in the reveal event?"

Danielle considered the question, absently swirling the wine in her glass. "Aimee's words, partly. But mostly... mostly it was seeing how proud you looked when I said I wanted to do it. Like you were proud to be with me, proud of what we have."

"I am proud. Incredibly proud," he said simply. He tucked a

curl behind her ear, fingertips lingering at the sensitive place just beneath it. "I want everyone to know how lucky I am that you chose me."

"I didn't choose you," she said softly. "We chose each other. Every day, in every conversation, in every letter we wrote before we knew who we were writing to."

The reminder of their anonymous correspondence seemed to deepen the intimacy between them. All those months of emotional vulnerability, of sharing thoughts and fears and dreams with someone they trusted but couldn't see—it had built a foundation that went deeper than physical attraction or casual dating.

"I have something for you," Darius said suddenly, setting down his wine glass and moving toward his bedroom.

"What kind of something?"

"The kind that's been waiting for the right moment."

He returned carrying a small wooden box that looked like it might be handmade. When he sat back down beside her, he was close enough that their knees touched, that she could feel the warmth radiating from his body.

"I've been working on this since we discovered each other's identities," he said, offering her the box with slightly nervous hands. "It's not much, but..."

Inside the box were letters—dozens of them, tied with ribbon and written in his familiar handwriting. But when she lifted the top one, she saw it was addressed to "My Dearest Danielle" rather than "Maplewood Muse."

"Letters I wrote to you after I knew who you were," he explained. "Things I wanted to say but didn't have the courage to. Thoughts about our future, about what you mean to me, about all the ways loving you has changed how I see everything."

Emotion clogged her throat as she held the collection of unsent letters. "Darius."

"I know we agreed to keep writing through the library

program, but I also wanted to have something that was just for you. Letters you could keep, that you could read whenever you wanted to remember how much I love you."

The thoughtfulness of the gesture, the time and care he'd put into creating something just for her, made tears gather in her eyes. "This is the most romantic thing anyone has ever done for me."

"You haven't read them yet. They might be terrible."

"They won't be terrible. They'll be you, which means they'll be perfect."

When she leaned forward to kiss him, it was with all the gratitude and love and overwhelming affection she couldn't put into words. His response was immediate and gentle, his hands coming up to frame her face as if she were something precious he was afraid of breaking.

"I love you," she whispered against his lips. "I love you so much it feels too big for my chest sometimes."

"I know the feeling," he murmured back, and then he was kissing her again, deeper this time, with a passion that spoke to months of building desire and emotional intimacy finally finding physical expression.

When they broke apart, both breathing hard, Danielle found herself studying his face in the soft lamplight. The strong line of his jaw, the way his eyes had gone dark with want, the slightly swollen state of his lips from their kisses.

"Darius," she said quietly, and something in her tone made his attention sharpen.

"What is it?"

"I want to stay tonight. I want to wake up next to you, want to see what this looks like in the morning light."

The expression that crossed his face was one of wonder mixed with desire and something deeper that might have been reverence.

"Are you sure?" he asked, though his hands were already

moving to her waist, pulling her closer. "Because once we cross this line, there's no going back for me."

"You're already it for me. This is just making it official," she said with a smile that felt radiant.

When he kissed her this time, it was with a passion that left no doubt about his feelings. His hands tangled in her hair while hers explored the broad expanse of his chest, both of them discovering the joy of finally being able to touch without reservation.

"Your bedroom," she managed to say between kisses. "Unless you want to scandalize your neighbors."

His laugh was low and delighted. "My bedroom it is."

He stood and offered her his hand, and when she took it, letting him pull her to her feet, she felt like she was stepping into her future. Every step toward his bedroom was deliberate, weighted with significance and anticipation.

At the threshold, he paused to look at her one more time. "Are you sure?"

Instead of answering with words, she reached up to begin unbuttoning his shirt, her fingers steady despite the excitement thrumming through her veins. "I've never been more sure of anything in my life."

The groan that rumbled from his chest was purely male satisfaction, and when he swept her up in his arms, carrying her the final few steps to his bed, she felt like the heroine of every romance novel she'd ever read.

"I love you," he said as he set her down gently beside the bed. "Whatever happens next, I need you to know that this isn't just physical for me. This is everything."

"It's everything for me too," she replied, reaching up to cup his face in her hands.

WHEN MORNING LIGHT filtered through his bedroom curtains, finding them tangled together in a peace she had ever experienced before, Danielle knew with absolute certainty that whatever challenges lay ahead, they would face them as partners in every sense of the word.

"Good morning, beautiful," Darius murmured against her hair, his arms tightening around her as consciousness returned.

"Good morning," she replied, pressing a soft kiss to his chest where her head rested. "How did you sleep?"

"Like a man who finally has everything he wants." He tilted her chin up so he could see her face. "You?"

"Like I finally found home."

They lay in comfortable silence for a while, watching dust motes dance in the morning sunlight and marveling at how right this felt. Eventually, Darius spoke again, his voice thoughtful.

"What are you thinking about?"

"The future," she admitted. "What comes next for us. Whether you'll get tired of having me around all the time."

"Never." His response was immediate and firm. "If anything, I'm already trying to figure out how to convince you to spend more time here. To make this..." He gestured around his small bedroom. "To make this ours instead of just mine."

The suggestion sent warmth flooding through her chest. "Are you asking me to move in with you?"

"Eventually. When you're ready. When it feels right." He pressed a kiss to the top of her head. "I'm not trying to rush anything, but I also don't want to pretend I don't want a future with you. A real future, with shared space and joint decisions and all the ordinary magic that comes with building a life together."

"I want that too," she said softly. "All of it. The ordinary and the magical and everything in between."

"Good," he said, and she could hear the smile in his voice.

"Because I'm planning to spend the rest of my life making sure you never regret saying yes to any of it."

As they eventually made their way to the kitchen for coffee and breakfast, moving around each other with a new ease and intimacy, Danielle felt like she was seeing her future clearly for the first time. It looked like Sunday mornings in rumpled pajamas, like shared books and quiet conversations, like someone who would love her through every season of life.

And if the universe had conspired to bring them together through anonymous letters and heated arguments about book displays, then she was grateful for every twist and turn that had led to this perfect morning, this perfect man, this perfect beginning of forever.

CHAPTER TWENTY

Danielle stood in front of her bedroom mirror Sunday morning, trying on her third outfit in fifteen minutes. She'd slipped out of Darius's apartment early to come home and get properly ready, though leaving his warm bed and sleepy kisses had been harder than she'd expected.

The navy dress felt too formal, the casual jeans seemed too relaxed, and now she was second-guessing the emerald green sweater and dark slacks she'd finally settled on.

"It's just my family," she muttered to her reflection, but even as she said it, she knew that wasn't entirely true. This was Darius meeting her family as her boyfriend—her serious, committed, I-love-you boyfriend. The man she'd spent the night with for the first time just a week ago, who'd made her coffee that morning wearing nothing but pajama pants and a smile that suggested he was remembering exactly how she'd ended up in his bed.

Her phone buzzed with a text from him:

Just finished getting the wine and flowers. Still nervous, but ready to charm the Jacobs family. See you in twenty minutes.

You don't need to charm anyone. Just be yourself. They're going to love you.

From your lips to God's ears. Though I have to admit, your father's approval means a lot to me.

The admission made her pulse quicken with affection. Darius cared about making a good impression because her family mattered to her, which meant they mattered to him. It was exactly the kind of thoughtfulness that had made her fall for him in the first place.

Twenty minutes later, she heard his car pull into her driveway. When she opened the door, he stood there holding a bouquet of fall flowers and looking devastatingly handsome in khakis and a navy button-down that brought out his eyes.

"These are for you," he said, offering the flowers with a slight smile. "And I have wine for your parents, though I wasn't sure what they prefer."

"They'll love whatever you brought. And you look perfect." She accepted the flowers, rising on her toes to kiss him hello.

"Ready to face the inquisition?" she asked as they walked to his car.

"Define ready."

"Prepared to answer questions about your intentions, your career prospects, and whether you're treating their baby daughter right."

"In that case, yes. I'm ready." He opened her car door with the gentlemanly courtesy that had become second nature. "Though I have to ask—how protective are we talking here?"

"Chrysta will interrogate you like you're applying for a

government job. Aleeyah will try to embarrass me with stories from our childhood. My father will want to know about your business plan and your long-term goals. And my mother will try to feed you until you can't move."

"And you think this will go well?"

Danielle settled into the passenger seat, watching him round the car with easy grace. "I think you're exactly the kind of man they've been hoping I'd find. You just have to let them see it."

The drive to her childhood home took fifteen minutes through tree-lined streets that showed off autumn's peak colors. As they pulled into the familiar driveway, Danielle felt the same mix of comfort and slight anxiety she always experienced during family gatherings.

"Last chance to run," she said as Darius turned off the engine.

"Not a chance. I've been looking forward to this since you first mentioned it."

The front door opened before they'd even reached the porch steps, and her mother appeared with the bright smile she reserved for special occasions and important guests.

"Danielle, sweetheart!" She enveloped her youngest daughter in a warm hug before turning expectant eyes to Darius. "And you must be Darius. We've heard so much about you."

"All good things, I hope," Darius replied, offering his hand with easy charm. "Thank you for having me, Mrs Jacobs. This is for you and Mr Jacobs." He presented a bottle of wine that he'd clearly chosen with care.

"Aren't you thoughtful! Come in, come in. Robert's in the living room, and the girls are in the kitchen helping with final preparations."

As they entered the familiar warmth of her childhood home, Danielle felt that unique combination of comfort and nervous energy that came with introducing someone important to the people who'd known her longest. The house smelled like her mother's famous pot roast and the apple pie that had been a Sunday tradition for as long as she could remember.

"Darius!" Aleeyah appeared from the kitchen, practically bouncing with excitement while balancing a one-year-old on her hip. "Finally! I was starting to think Danielle was making you up."

"Very real and very happy to meet you properly," Darius said, accepting Aleeyah's enthusiastic one-armed hug with good humor before turning his attention to the little girl who was studying him with serious dark eyes. "And you must be Zara. Your aunt has told me so much about you."

The toddler hid her face against her mother's shoulder with shy curiosity.

"She's usually more social than this," Aleeyah said with a laugh. "But she's at that age where strangers make her cautious. Zara, can you say hi to Aunt Danielle's boyfriend?"

Zara peeked out at Darius, then reached toward Danielle with grabby hands and a delighted squeal of "Dani!"

"There's my favorite niece," Danielle said, taking the little girl and settling her on her hip with practiced ease. "Zara, this is Darius. He's very nice."

"Where is Greg?" Danielle asked, looking around the living room that felt exactly the same as it had throughout her childhood.

"Kitchen, helping Mom with last-minute preparations and probably sneaking tastes of everything," Aleeyah replied. "And Chrysta's in there too with Terrence. Fair warning—she's in full protective mode."

Danielle felt Darius's hand find hers, squeezing gently. "They mean well," she assured him quietly. "They just want to make sure you're worthy of their baby sister."

"Am I?" he asked, meeting her eyes with an expression that was both playful and serious.

"Definitely."

Her father appeared from his study, extending a firm handshake to Darius with the assessing look.

"So you're the young man who's been making our Danielle so happy," he said, his tone friendly but unmistakably evaluative. "I'm Robert Jacobs."

"Darius Jones, sir. It's an honor to meet you."

"The bookstore owner," her father said approvingly. "I respect a man who works with books. Shows character and intellectual depth."

As they moved toward the kitchen, Danielle caught Darius's slight smile at her father's immediate approval. The kitchen was bustling with controlled chaos—her mother directing operations while Chrysta arranged appetizers and Greg helped set the dining room table. Terrence stood near the counter looking completely at ease in the family mayhem, bearing witness to how well he'd integrated into their Sunday dinner tradition.

"And here's the famous Darius!" Chrysta announced, looking up from her cheese and crackers arrangement with obvious curiosity. "I'm Chrysta, the older sister and self-appointed family protector."

"Should I be worried?" Darius asked with amusement, glancing at Danielle.

"Only if your intentions aren't honorable," Chrysta replied with a grin that took some of the sting out of her words. "Though from what I hear, you're more of the strong, silent type who wins hearts through literary debates and anonymous love letters."

Heat crept up Danielle's neck. "Chrysta—"

"What? It's romantic! You argued about book displays and fell in love through secret correspondence. It's like something out of a Jane Austen novel."

"With better communication skills," Greg added, approaching with an extended hand and a welcoming smile.

As the introductions continued around the kitchen, Danielle

watched Darius relax into the easy rhythm of her family's conversation. He complimented her mother's cooking with genuine appreciation, discussed local business challenges with her father, and listened with obvious interest as Aleeyah described her recent adventures in married life.

"So," Chrysta said as they settled around the familiar dining room table, "we need to hear the whole story. From the beginning. Danielle's been frustratingly vague about important details."

"I have not been vague—"

"You told us you were corresponding with someone called Evergreen and dating a bookstore owner, but you somehow failed to mention they were the same person for weeks," Aleeyah pointed out with sisterly directness. "That's extremely vague."

Darius reached for Danielle's hand under the table, squeezing gently as he answered. "It was complicated for us too. We were falling for each other in two different ways without realizing it."

"Tell us about the letters," her mother encouraged, settling back in her chair with the expression of someone preparing to hear a romantic story. "How did you know she was special?"

"From her very first response," Darius replied without hesitation, his voice carrying the warmth of genuine affection. "She wrote about finding human stories in data analysis, about seeing beauty and meaning in everyday work that other people dismiss as mundane. Her perspective was thoughtful, challenging, completely authentic. I found myself looking forward to her letters more than anything else in my week."

"And you had no idea it was Danielle?"

"Not until the coincidences became impossible to ignore. We kept having parallel experiences—she'd mention encounters about literature accessibility, I'd write about learning to share my love of books more generously. The timing, the insights, the way our thoughts seemed to complement each other..." He paused, glancing at Danielle with an expression that made her heart skip. "It was like we were having the same conversations in two different formats."

"It was exactly like that," Danielle added, warming to the subject despite her earlier embarrassment. "In person, we'd argue about his pretentious book displays. In letters, we'd explore what it means to make literature accessible without compromising its value."

"Pretentious?" her father asked with obvious amusement.

"His original window display was intimidating leather-bound classics and dense literary theory," Danielle explained, shooting Darius an affectionate look. "I may have told him he was gatekeeping literature instead of inviting people in."

"She was absolutely right," Darius admitted readily. "Though I didn't appreciate being called out at the time. I was so focused on preserving what I thought was important about books that I'd forgotten why they're actually important—to connect people, to tell stories that matter, to make readers feel less alone in the world."

"And now?" Terrence asked, joining the conversation with obvious interest.

"Now I realize that the best criticism comes from people who care enough to challenge you when you're wrong." Darius's eyes found Danielle's across the table, and his voice carried a weight that made her pulse flutter. "She made me a better book-store owner and a better person."

The warmth in his voice, the way he was looking at her like she'd given him something precious, made Danielle's chest feel tight with affection.

"What about you, Danielle?" her mother asked gently. "When did you know he was special?"

"When I realized I was looking forward to arguing with him as much as I looked forward to Evergreen's letters," she replied honestly, her fingers tightening around Darius's hand. "Most people either dismiss my opinions or agree with everything I say to avoid conflict. Darius actually listened, considered my perspective, and wasn't afraid to push back when he disagreed. It made every conversation feel important."

"Plus he's supporting her writing career," Chrysta added with obvious approval. "That's not nothing in my book."

"The poetry readings at the bookstore were Darius's idea," Danielle explained, feeling proud and slightly embarrassed in equal measure. "He's been encouraging me to take my writing seriously since before we were even dating."

"Because your writing matters," Darius said simply, his tone carrying the same conviction she'd heard in his letters. "You see connections other people miss, find beauty in places others overlook. That perspective is worth sharing with the world."

The dinner conversation flowed naturally from there, touching on everything from Darius's expansion plans for the bookstore to Danielle's recent freelance writing successes. Her family peppered him with questions about his background, his goals, his family, his intentions—all delivered with the loving nosiness she'd grown up with but had forgotten could feel over-whelming to outsiders.

"So what are your plans for the bookstore long-term?" her father asked as they shared her mother's apple pie. "Small businesses can be challenging in today's economy."

"I'm working on expanding our community programming," Darius replied thoughtfully. "Poetry readings, book clubs for different age groups, writing workshops. The goal is to make it more of a cultural center than just a retail space. Literature is most powerful when it brings people together."

"That sounds like a solid business model. Community engagement builds customer loyalty."

"It also builds something more important than profit," Darius said, his passion for his work evident in his voice. "It builds connection. People need places where they can share ideas, discover new perspectives, feel part of something larger than themselves."

Her father nodded approvingly. "You sound like a man who understands the value of community."

"I'm learning to. Danielle's taught me a lot about seeing beyond my own assumptions and really listening to what people need."

As the evening continued with coffee and more conversation in the living room, Danielle found herself curled against Darius's side on the familiar couch, listening to him discuss local history with her father while her sisters peppered him with questions about rare book collecting and the challenges of running a small business.

"He fits," her mother said quietly, settling beside Danielle while the men were distracted by a debate about historical preservation.

"He does," Danielle agreed, watching Darius gesture animatedly as he described a first-edition discovery he'd made at an estate sale. "Better than I expected."

"You look happy, sweetheart. Really, genuinely happy in a way I haven't seen since you were a little girl discovering something new."

"I am happy. Happier than I knew I could be." She met her mother's eyes, seeing the approval and maternal satisfaction there. "I didn't realize how much I needed someone who saw all of me—the analytical side and the creative side, the confident parts and the uncertain parts—and valued it all equally."

"That's what the right person does. They don't ask you to choose between parts of yourself or become someone different to earn their love."

As the evening wound down and they prepared to leave, Danielle felt the deep satisfaction of a milestone successfully reached. Her family had welcomed Darius with genuine warmth, and he'd handled their enthusiasm and protective questioning with exactly the right balance of respect and humor.

"Walk me to the car?" her father asked Darius quietly as they gathered coats and said goodbyes. It was phrased as a request, but Danielle recognized the tone that meant her father had something specific to discuss.

"Of course, sir," Darius replied, though she caught the slight tension in his shoulders that suggested he understood the significance of the invitation.

Through the front window, she watched them have what appeared to be a serious but friendly conversation beside Darius's car. Her father was gesturing with the measured authority of someone making important points, while Darius listened with the focused attention of someone who understood he was being evaluated for something significant.

"What do you think they're talking about?" Aleeyah asked, joining her at the window.

"Dad's probably giving him the 'treat my daughter right or answer to me' speech," Chrysta said with amusement. "Though honestly, if he can't see how much that man adores Danielle, he needs his eyes checked."

When they returned to the house, both men looked satisfied with whatever had been discussed. Her father shook Darius's hand with obvious warmth, and Darius's expression carried a contentment that suggested the conversation had gone well.

"Ready to go?" he asked, approaching Danielle with a smile that seemed different somehow—more settled, more certain.

"More than ready."

The drive home was filled with comfortable conversation about the evening, though Danielle noticed Darius seemed more thoughtful than usual, as if he was processing something important.

"They love you," she said as they pulled up behind the bookstore. "My father especially. I could tell by the way he relaxed after talking to you."

"Your family is wonderful. I can see where you get your passion and your determination." He turned off the engine but made no move to get out of the car. "And your willingness to call people on their assumptions."

"What did my father say to you outside?"

Darius was quiet for a moment, his hands still resting on the steering wheel. "He told me he could see how much I care about you. And he said that anyone who could make his daughter this happy was welcome in the family."

"That's all?"

"He also said he trusted me to take care of you, and that he hoped I understood what a gift it was to be loved by someone like you." Darius turned to face her fully, his expression serious and tender. "He's right. It is a gift. The greatest one I've ever received."

The words sent warmth flooding through her chest. "I love you too. And they love you, which means Sunday dinners are going to become a regular thing. We can alternate between your family and mine."

"I'm looking forward to it. To all of it—the family dinners, the debates about literature, the way your mother tries to feed me enough food for three people." He reached over to take her hand. "To building a life with you that includes all the people we care about."

As they climbed the stairs to his apartment, Danielle felt like they'd crossed another important threshold. Meeting the family was serious business in the Jacobs household, and the fact that Darius had not only passed their collective inspection but genuinely seemed to enjoy their company felt significant.

"Thank you," she said as they settled on his couch with cups of tea. "For being so perfect tonight, for winning them over, for making the whole thing feel easy when it could have been terrifying."

"Thank you for wanting me to meet them. For including me in your family." He pulled her closer, pressing a soft kiss to the top of her head. "Tonight just made me more certain than ever that I want to be part of your life in every possible way."

"You already are," she said softly, settling against his side with the contentment of someone who'd found exactly where she belonged. "You have been since that first letter."

And as they sat together in the quiet of his apartment, Danielle felt like they were building something solid and lasting —not just romance, but partnership. The kind of love that could weather family scrutiny and community attention, that could grow stronger with every shared experience and every challenge they faced together.

It was exactly what she'd been hoping to find when she'd signed up for that pen-pal program. She just hadn't known then that it would come packaged with Sunday dinners and protective fathers and the deep satisfaction of watching the man she loved fit seamlessly into the life she'd built.

CHAPTER TWENTY-ONE

Darius sat in his grandmother's living room Wednesday evening, the small velvet box burning a hole in his jacket pocket as he tried to focus on her story about the church quilting circle's latest drama. His grandmother had been talking for twenty minutes about Mrs Henderson's controversial fabric choices, but all he could think about was the ring hidden just inches from his heart and the conversation he needed to have with her.

The ring had belonged to his grandmother's mother—a simple but elegant solitaire that caught light beautifully without being ostentatious. When he'd asked his grandmother if he could offer it to Danielle, she'd cried and pressed it into his hands with the fierce joy of someone who'd been waiting years for this moment.

"That ring has been sitting in my jewelry box for fifteen years, just waiting for the right woman," she'd said, dabbing at her eyes with a handkerchief. "The moment I met Danielle, I knew she was the one it was meant for."

Now, three days later, he was finally ready to share his plan with the woman who'd essentially raised him after his parents moved to Atlanta. His grandmother had always been his sounding board for important decisions, and proposing to the love of his life definitely qualified as important.

"Grandma," he said during a lull in her quilting circle commentary, "I need to tell you something."

"I was wondering when you'd get around to it," she said with the knowing smile that suggested she'd been waiting for this conversation since he'd arrived. "You've been fidgeting with your jacket pocket for the past half hour."

Heat crept up his neck. "Am I that obvious?"

"Only to someone who's been watching you grow up. When are you planning to ask her?"

The question he'd been both anticipating and dreading hung in the air between them. "Friday night. At the pen-pal reveal event."

His grandmother's eyebrows rose with interest. "Now that's romantic. Where you two found each other in the first place."

"Mrs Williams has been after us to participate for months, and we finally agreed. I figure if we're going to share our story publicly anyway, why not make it even more meaningful?" He pulled the ring box from his pocket, turning it over in his hands. "I've been carrying this around for a week, waiting for the right moment."

"And you think Friday night is the right moment?"

"I think any moment I get to tell Danielle I want to spend the rest of my life with her is the right moment," he said quietly. "But yes, there's something perfect about proposing in front of the community that brought us together. All those people who've been invested in our story from the beginning."

His grandmother leaned forward in her chair, studying his face with the shrewd attention that had made her an excellent high school principal for thirty years. "Are you nervous?"

"Terrified," he admitted. "Not about her answer—I know she loves me. But about everything that comes after. Marriage, building a life together, making decisions that affect both of us for the next fifty years."

"That's smart terror. The kind that means you understand what you're asking for." She reached over to pat his hand. "Tell me what you're thinking about when you imagine your future with her."

Darius set the ring box on the coffee table between them and leaned back in his chair, letting himself really consider the question. "I think about Sunday mornings reading together in bed. I think about her helping customers at the bookstore, the way she connects with people and makes them feel seen. I think about supporting her writing career and watching her confidence grow as more people discover her work."

He paused, gathering his thoughts. "I think about disagreeing with her about everything from book displays to dinner plans, but knowing we'll always work it out because we respect each other enough to listen. I think about her challenging me to be better while accepting me exactly as I am."

"What about children?"

The question he'd been avoiding thinking about too deeply sent a flutter of anticipation through his chest. "I think about that too. She'd be an incredible mother—patient, thoughtful, the kind of parent who encourages questions and supports dreams. And watching her with little Zara last Sunday..." He trailed off, remembering how natural she'd looked with her niece on her hip, how easily she'd moved between adult conversation and toddler entertainment.

"She'd want children?"

"We haven't talked about it specifically, but I think so. The way she lights up around Zara, the way she talks about her students when she volunteers at the library's reading program— she loves nurturing people, helping them grow." He met his grandmother's eyes. "I want to give her everything she wants,

Grandma. Children, a bigger house if she wants one, travel, financial security to pursue her writing without worry."

"And what do you want from her?"

The question caught him off guard with its directness. "Her. Just her, exactly as she is. Her thoughts, her laugh, her way of seeing stories everywhere. I want to wake up next to her every morning and fall asleep holding her every night. I want to be the person she comes to with good news and bad news, the one she trusts with her fears and her dreams."

His grandmother's smile was radiant. "Then you're ready."

"How do you know?"

"Because you're not thinking about what marriage will give you—you're thinking about what you can give to each other. That's the foundation of every lasting partnership."

They talked for another hour about practical details—how he planned to surprise her during their presentation, what he'd say, how he thought she'd react. His grandmother shared stories about his grandfather's proposal fifty-five years ago, about the early years of their marriage and the lessons they'd learned about choosing each other daily.

"Marriage isn't about the wedding or the proposal or even the honeymoon," she said as he prepared to leave. "It's about Tuesday mornings when you're both tired and stressed, and you still choose kindness. It's about supporting each other's dreams even when they don't align perfectly with your own plans."

"Did you ever doubt your choice? About Grandpa, I mean."

"Every marriage has moments of doubt, honey. Moments when you remember you chose to tie your life to another flawed human being who will sometimes disappoint you." She paused, her expression growing thoughtful. "But doubt and regret are different things. I never regretted choosing your grandfather, even during our hardest times."

The distinction resonated with Darius as he drove home through the quiet streets of Sweetgum. He'd had moments of doubt about whether he was ready for marriage, whether he could be the partner Danielle deserved, whether they were moving too fast. But he'd never regretted falling in love with her, never questioned whether she was the right person for him.

Back in his apartment, he placed the ring box on his bedside table and tried to imagine Friday night. He'd already confirmed the details with Mrs Williams—they'd be the final couple to share their story, giving him the perfect opportunity to transition from their presentation to his proposal. The community center would be full of people who'd been cheering for their relationship from the beginning, creating exactly the kind of supportive atmosphere he wanted for this moment.

His phone buzzed with a text from Danielle:

> Just finished my presentation notes for Friday. Are you nervous about speaking in front of everyone?

> A little.

He typed back, which was both true and a massive under-statement.

> But mostly excited to share our story.

She replied,

> I love that we get to do this together. That we get to tell people how much the program meant to us.

> It gave me everything I didn't know I was looking for.

He replied, thinking about the ring waiting just feet away.

Me too. See you tomorrow? I was thinking we could practice our presentation over dinner.

Perfect. I'll cook.

As he set his phone aside and began preparing for bed, Darius felt a deep sense of rightness about his decision. Proposing to Danielle at the pen-pal reveal event wasn't just romantic—it was honest. Their love story had begun with community support, had weathered community attention, and had grown stronger through the foundation of shared values and authentic communication that Mrs Williams' program had fostered.

Friday night, he would stand in front of everyone who mattered to them and ask Danielle to marry him. He would promise to love her through every season of life, to support her dreams and share his own, to choose her again and again no matter what challenges they faced.

And if the universe had orchestrated their meeting through anonymous letters and heated arguments about book accessibility, then he was grateful for every twist and turn that had led to this moment of absolute certainty about their future together.

Thursday evening, Danielle arrived at his apartment with the kind of nervous energy that suggested she was taking their upcoming presentation seriously. They spent two hours crafting their remarks, deciding how much of their story to share and how to frame their experience in ways that might help other people believe in the possibility of unexpected love.

"I think we should mention how we almost didn't participate," Danielle said as they sat at his small dining table with their notes spread between them. "How we were afraid of being on display, but then realized we wanted to honor what brought us together."

"And how the program taught us that the best relationships

require vulnerability and patience," Darius added, though his mind was already racing ahead to what he planned to say after their official presentation ended.

"Are you ready for this? For everyone to know our business?"

"I'm ready for everyone to know how much I love you," he said, reaching across to take her hand. "Beyond that, their opinions don't matter."

The simple declaration seemed to settle something in her expression. "I love you too. More than I ever thought I could love anyone."

As they practiced their presentation, Darius found himself memorizing details he wanted to remember forever—the way Danielle's eyes lit up when she talked about their early letters, the thoughtful pauses she took while considering how to phrase their more intimate revelations, the pride in her voice when she described how he'd changed his approach to the bookstore.

Friday morning, he woke with anticipation thrumming through his veins. Today was the day he would ask the woman he loved to marry him. Today was the day their story would officially begin its next chapter.

The ring box sat on his dresser, catching morning light and throwing tiny rainbows across the wall. In twelve hours, he would be on one knee in front of their entire community, offering Danielle a future that he hoped would exceed even her most romantic expectations.

And if his hands were shaking slightly as he got dressed for work, if his heart was already racing with the magnitude of what he was about to do, then it was simply proof of how much this moment—and this woman—meant to him.

Tonight, everything would change. Tonight, he would ask Danielle Jacobs to become Danielle Jones, and their anonymous correspondence would transform into a lifetime of love letters written in the language of shared dreams and daily devotion.

He couldn't wait.

CHAPTER TWENTY-TWO

Darius stood in the men's room of the Sweetgum Community Center Friday evening, staring at his reflection while trying to calm his racing heart. The ring box felt impossibly heavy in his jacket pocket, and he'd checked at least six times in the past hour to make sure it was still there. Through the door, he could hear the murmur of conversation as community members took their seats for the pen-pal reveal event.

"You can do this," he whispered to his reflection. "Just get through the presentation, then ask the woman you love to marry you in front of everyone you know. Simple."

The irony of his nerves wasn't lost on him. He'd spoken in front of academic conferences, had defended his thesis to a panel of intimidating professors, had given presentations to potential investors for the bookstore. But none of that compared to the terror and excitement of what he was about to do.

A knock on the door interrupted his pep talk. "Darius? You okay in there?" Danielle's voice carried concern and affection in equal measure.

"Just fixing my tie," he called back, though his tie had been perfectly straight for the past ten minutes.

"Mrs Williams wants to go over the schedule one more time before we start. We're up last, remember?"

"I'll be right out."

He took one final look in the mirror, straightened his shoulders, and checked the ring box one last time. Tonight was the night he'd been planning for weeks, the night that would change everything.

When he emerged from the restroom, Danielle was waiting in the hallway looking radiant in a burgundy dress that complemented her warm brown eyes and dark hair. The sight of her sent his pulse skittering, as it had every day since he'd first seen her argue with him about book displays.

"You look beautiful," he said, reaching for her hand with fingers that weren't entirely steady.

"You look nervous," she replied, studying his face with the perceptiveness that had drawn him to her letters in the first place.

"I want tonight to be perfect. For us, for the program, for everyone who's been supporting us."

The answer seemed to satisfy her, though she continued to watch him with curious eyes as they walked toward the main hall. "It will be perfect. We're telling our story, honoring what brought us together. What could be more perfect than that?"

If only she knew, Darius thought, the ring box seeming to pulse against his chest with every heartbeat.

The community center's main hall had been transformed for the occasion. Round tables decorated with books and flowers filled the space, while a small platform at the front held a podium and microphone. At least fifty people had turned out for the event—couples from the pen-pal program, library supporters, friends and family members who'd been following various love stories with invested interest.

Darius spotted his grandparents at a front table, his grandmother catching his eye and giving him an encouraging nod that somehow steadied his nerves. Danielle's family occupied another front table, little Zara on Aleeyah's lap clapping her hands at the twinkling lights that decorated the room.

"Look at all these people," Danielle murmured as they found their reserved seats. "I can't believe this many people care about anonymous letter writing."

"They care about love stories," Darius corrected gently. "And hope. And the idea that meaningful connections can happen in unexpected ways."

Mrs Williams took the podium with obvious joy, welcoming everyone and explaining how the evening would unfold. Five couples would share their experiences with the pen-pal program, describing how written correspondence had led to friendship, romance, and in some cases, lasting partnership.

The first couple, both in their seventies, had reconnected through letters after being widowed and finding companionship in shared memories of long marriages. The second pair, barely out of college, had discovered they lived three blocks away despite attending universities in different states. Each story was unique.

As the evening progressed, Darius found himself both captivated by the other stories and increasingly nervous about their own presentation. The ring box felt like it was broadcasting his intentions to the entire room, though logically he knew no one could see it beneath his jacket.

"We're next," Danielle whispered as the fourth couple concluded their remarks to warm applause.

"Ready?" he asked, though he suspected she could hear the strain in his voice.

"With you? Always."

Mrs Williams introduced them with obvious pride, describing their story as "a perfect example of how letters can bridge any gap, even the one between two people who thought they already knew each other."

As they approached the podium together, Darius was hyper-aware of every detail—the warm lighting, the expectant faces in the audience, the way Danielle's hand felt in his as they climbed the few steps to the platform. This was it.

"Thank you all for being here tonight," Danielle began, her voice carrying clearly through the room despite her earlier nervousness. "When we first signed up for Mrs Williams' pen-pal program, neither of us expected to find love. We were looking for intellectual stimulation, meaningful conversation, authentic connection in a world that often feels focused on surface-level interaction."

"What we found was each other," Darius continued, his voice steadying as he fell into the rhythm they'd practiced. "Though it took us a while to realize it. We were falling in love through letters while arguing about literature in person."

A ripple of laughter moved through the audience, and Darius felt some of his tension ease. These were their friends, their community, people who'd been invested in their happiness from the beginning.

"Our correspondence taught us that real intimacy requires vulnerability," Danielle said, glancing at him with an expression of such love that his breath caught. "That the best relationships are built on honest communication, even when that communication challenges our assumptions about ourselves and the world."

"It also taught us that sometimes the people who irritate us most are the ones we're meant to care about most," Darius added, earning another laugh from the audience. "That genuine compatibility isn't about finding someone who agrees with everything we think—it's about finding someone who sees us clearly and chooses us anyway."

They shared more details about their correspondence, about

the gradual realization that their anonymous pen pal and their real-life sparring partner were the same person. The audience was completely engaged, murmuring appreciation at the more romantic details and nodding recognition at the universal truths about love and connection.

"But the program gave us more than just each other," Danielle continued, nearing the end of their prepared remarks. "It reminded us that meaningful relationships require intention, patience, and the willingness to be vulnerable with another person."

"Which brings me to something I need to say," Darius said, his heart hammering as he deviated from their script. "Something I need to say publicly, in front of this community that's supported us from the beginning."

He turned to face Danielle fully, noting the confusion that flickered across her features as she realized he was going off-script. The room had gone completely quiet, everyone sensing that something significant was about to happen.

"Danielle, these past months with you have shown me what it means to be truly known by another person. You've challenged me to be better, supported my dreams, and somehow managed to love both the man I am and the man I'm becoming."

Her eyes widened as understanding began to dawn, her hand flying to her mouth as he reached into his jacket pocket.

"You've taught me that the best love stories aren't about finding someone perfect—they're about finding someone perfect for you. Someone who sees your flaws and loves you not despite them, but because they're part of what makes you who you are."

He pulled out the ring box, and the audience's collective gasp was audible as he dropped to one knee right there on the platform, in front of everyone they knew.

"I know this isn't how most people propose," he said, opening the box to reveal his great-grandmother's ring in the twinkling lights. "But our story began with this community's support, and it feels right to take this step with all of you as witnesses."

Tears were streaming down Danielle's face now, her free hand pressed to her chest as if to contain her racing heart. Around them, the room was utterly silent, everyone holding their breath for her answer.

"Danielle Jacobs, you are my favorite argument, my deepest conversation, my truest friend, and the love I never knew I was looking for." His voice was steady despite the emotion threatening to overwhelm him. "Will you marry me?"

The words hung in the air between them, weighted with all the love and hope and certainty he'd been carrying for weeks. For a moment that felt like eternity, she simply stared at him with tears streaming down her face and wonder shining in her eyes.

Then she was launching herself into his arms, nearly knocking him backward as she wrapped her arms around his neck.

"Yes," she said, her voice breaking with joy. "Yes, absolutely yes, of course yes!"

The room erupted in applause and cheers as Darius stood, lifting her off her feet and spinning her around while she laughed and cried simultaneously. When he set her down and slipped the ring onto her finger with hands that trembled with relief and happiness, the standing ovation grew even louder.

"I love you," she whispered against his lips as he kissed her with all the passion and promise he'd been holding back. "I love you so much, and yes, yes, I want to marry you."

"I love you too," he murmured back, framing her face with his hands and marveling that she'd said yes, that this incredible woman had agreed to spend her life with him. "Forever, Danielle. In every way that matters."

When they finally broke apart, still holding each other close, the applause had evolved into laughter and tears from their audience. Mrs Williams was dabbing at her eyes with a handkerchief, his grandmother was beaming with satisfaction, and Danielle's family was embracing each other with obvious joy.

"Well," Mrs Williams said into her microphone, her voice thick with emotion, "I think that's the most beautiful testimonial we could have asked for."

More applause filled the room as they made their way back to their table, stopping every few steps to accept congratulations and well-wishes from other attendees. The ring caught the light every time Danielle moved her hand, and she kept staring at it with wonder, as if she couldn't quite believe it was real.

"Did you plan this the whole time?" she asked as they finally reached their seats, both still glowing with happiness.

"For weeks. I've been carrying that ring around, waiting for the perfect moment."

"And you thought the perfect moment was in front of fifty people?"

"I thought the perfect moment was whenever I got to tell you I want to spend my life with you," he said, bringing her hand to his lips to press a soft kiss just above the ring. "But yes, there was something perfect about doing it here, where our story began."

The rest of the evening passed in a blur of congratulations and celebration. Other couples approached to share their own engagement stories, elderly women offered unsolicited advice about wedding planning, and children from the audience asked to see the ring up close. Through it all, Darius found himself marveling at how right this felt—not just the proposal, but the community response, the shared joy, the sense that their love story belonged to more people than just the two of them.

"I can't believe you kept this secret," Danielle said as they drove home later, her left hand catching streetlight every time she gestured. "How long have you been planning this?"

"Since our dinner with your family. Actually, if I'm being honest, probably since the night you agreed to participate in tonight's event. I realized it would be the perfect opportunity to honor where we started while stepping into where we're going.

As they pulled up behind the bookstore—their bookstore, their home, their future—Danielle turned to face him with an expression of such radiant happiness that it took his breath away.

"So what happens now?" she asked. "Besides the obvious wedding planning and figuring out if I'm moving in here officially."

"Now we start the next chapter," Darius said, bringing her hand to his lips again. "The one where we stop dating and start being engaged. The one where we plan a wedding and a honeymoon and all the adventures we want to have together."

"And after that?"

"After that, we keep choosing each other. Every day, for the rest of our lives."

As they climbed the stairs to his apartment—their apartment, he realized, since she'd been spending most nights there anyway—Danielle paused on the landing to look at the ring again.

"It's perfect," she said softly. "Where did you find it?"

"It was my great-grandmother's. My grandmother gave it to me when I told her I wanted to propose. She said it had been waiting fifteen years for the right woman."

"And she thought I was the right woman?"

"She knew you were the right woman the moment she met you. She said you saw me clearly and loved what you saw, and that was rare enough to be treasured."

Inside the apartment, they settled on the couch, both still

processing the magnitude of what had just happened. Danielle kept looking at the ring, turning her hand to catch the light, smiling with the kind of joy that seemed to radiate from her entire being.

"I have a confession," she said after a while.

"What's that?"

"I've been hoping you'd propose. Ever since that Sunday dinner with my family, actually. The way you looked when my father was talking to you, the way you seemed so settled about us..." She shrugged, looking slightly embarrassed. "I started imagining what it would be like to be your wife instead of just your girlfriend."

"And what did you imagine?"

"Waking up next to you every morning for the rest of my life. Sharing holidays with both our families. Supporting each other through whatever challenges come our way." She paused, meeting his eyes with an expression that made his heart skip. "Maybe eventually adding to our family, if you want children."

"I do want children. With you, someday, when we're ready."

"Good," she said, settling against his side with the contentment of someone who'd found exactly where she belonged. "Because I want to give you everything you've dreamed of, just like you've given me everything I never knew I wanted."

As they sat together planning their future—discussing wedding dates and guest lists and where they wanted to honeymoon—Darius felt the profound satisfaction of a life clicking into perfect focus. Tomorrow they would start the practical work of planning a wedding, but tonight was for celebrating the decision to build a life together.

And if the universe had conspired to bring them together through anonymous letters and heated arguments about literature, then he was grateful for every twist and turn that had led to this perfect evening, this perfect woman, this perfect beginning of forever.

Because the best love stories, he'd learned, were the ones that surprised you by being exactly what you needed—delivered in ways you never could have predicted, but recognized the moment they appeared. And theirs, he knew with absolute certainty, was going to be worth living for a lifetime.

EPILOGUE

Six months later, Danielle stood in the bridal suite of Sweetgum Community Center, staring at her reflection in the full-length mirror that Chrysta had insisted on bringing. The ivory dress she'd chosen was simple but elegant, with delicate lace sleeves and a flowing skirt that made her feel like the heroine of every romance novel she'd ever read. Her grandmother's pearl necklace—something borrowed—caught the spring sunlight streaming through the windows.

"You look perfect," Aleeyah said, adjusting the delicate veil that had been their mother's. "Absolutely radiant."

"I can't believe you're actually getting married," Chrysta added, dabbing at her eyes with a tissue while one-year-old Zara tugged at her aunt's dress with fascinated determination. "It feels like yesterday you were complaining about being the only single sister."

Danielle laughed, smoothing her hands over the dress one final time. "It feels like yesterday I was arguing with Darius about pretentious book displays. Now look at us."

Through the window, she could see guests arriving for their ceremony. Darius's parents had driven down from Atlanta, his college friends had made the trip, and what seemed like half of Sweetgum had turned out to celebrate their local love story. Mrs Williams bustled around directing ushers with military precision, while the hit-and-run squad supervised flower arrangements with obvious satisfaction at their matchmaking success.

"Are you nervous?" Aleeyah asked, noting how Danielle kept glancing toward the door.

"Not about marrying him," Danielle said without hesitation. "Just about not tripping during the processional in front of everyone we know."

A soft knock interrupted them, and Darius's grandmother peered around the door. "May I come in? I have something for the bride."

She entered carrying a small wrapped box, her eyes bright with tears of joy. "This is from Darius and me—well, mostly from me, but he approved."

Inside the box was a delicate silver bracelet with a small charm shaped like an open book.

"It's beautiful," Danielle breathed, holding it up to catch the light.

"Read the inscription," his grandmother said with a knowing smile.

Danielle turned the charm over to read the tiny engraving: "Every love story deserves a beautiful beginning." - E and M M

"Evergreen and Maplewood Muse," she whispered, feeling tears threaten her carefully applied makeup.

"He wanted you to have something that honored how you found each other, but also looked forward to all the chapters you haven't written yet."

As his grandmother fastened the bracelet around her wrist, Danielle felt a warmth that had nothing to do with the spring sunshine. This was what she'd been hoping for since that first pen-pal letter—someone who saw her completely and chose to love all of it, someone who understood that the best relationships were built on daily kindness and ongoing choice.

"Time to go," Chrysta announced, checking her phone. "The groom is getting antsy, according to his best man."

The processional was everything Danielle had hoped for—simple, elegant, and focused on what mattered. She walked down the aisle on her father's arm to find Darius waiting at the front, looking devastatingly handsome in his navy suit and absolutely radiant with happiness.

When their eyes met, everything else faded away—the assembled guests, the photographer, even her nervousness about speaking in public. There was only Darius, looking at her like she was the answer to every question he'd ever asked.

"Hi," he whispered as her father placed her hand in his.

"Hi," she whispered back, and they both smiled at the simplicity of it.

The ceremony was brief but meaningful, officiated by the Pastor, who'd known both families for years. They'd written their own vows, keeping them private until this moment.

"Danielle," Darius began, his voice steady despite the emotion in his brown eyes, "you taught me that the best arguments are the ones that lead to understanding, and the best love is the one that challenges us to grow. You've made me braver about sharing what I love, more generous with my heart, and absolutely certain that some people are worth rearranging your whole life around."

"Darius," Danielle replied, her voice thick with tears she'd promised herself she wouldn't cry, "you showed me that it's possible to be completely known and completely loved at the same time. You've supported my dreams, celebrated my successes, and made me believe that I deserve a love that sees all of me and chooses all of me, every single day."

The exchange of rings was accompanied by promises that

felt both monumental and natural—the formal declaration of what they'd been living for months.

"By the power vested in me by the state of Georgia," the Pastor announced with obvious joy, "I now pronounce you husband and wife. Darius, you may kiss your bride."

The kiss was soft, sweet, and accompanied by applause from everyone who'd been invested in their love story from its argumentative beginning. When they broke apart, both grinning, Danielle felt like she was looking at her future and finding it exactly right.

The reception was held in the community center's main hall, decorated with books and flowers in a nod to how they'd met. The hit-and-run squad had outdone themselves with coordination, Mrs Williams had provided a cake that somehow managed to incorporate both literary quotes and mathematical symbols, and Darius's grandmother had planned a menu that satisfied everyone from vegetarians to devoted meat-eaters.

"Speech! Speech!" someone called as they finished their first dance to a song Darius had chosen based on a poem Danielle had written about finding love in unexpected places.

Darius helped Danielle onto the small platform they'd used for the ceremony, both of them looking out at the assembled group of family and friends who'd supported their relationship from its earliest days.

"We want to thank everyone for being here," Danielle began, her voice carrying clearly through the room. "When I signed up for Mrs Williams's pen-pal program, I was looking for meaningful conversation. I never expected to find my best friend, my greatest challenge, and the love of my life all in the same person."

"And when I challenged Danielle's opinions about book displays," Darius continued, "I thought I was defending literature. I never expected to meet someone who would teach me what literature is actually for—connecting hearts across any distance, even the one between two stubborn people who thought they already knew everything."

"We also want to thank this community for believing in love stories, even when they start with arguments and involve anonymous letters," Danielle added. "Your investment in our happiness means more than you know."

"And Mrs Everly Williams," Darius said, raising his glass toward the librarian, "thank you for creating a program that proves sometimes the best way to find someone is to stop looking and start being honest about who you are."

The applause was warm and sustained, but it was the expressions on their guests' faces that moved Danielle most—genuine joy at seeing two people find exactly what they'd been looking for in each other.

As the evening continued with dancing, conversation, and the kind of celebration that made small-town life feel rich and meaningful, Danielle found quiet moments to appreciate how far they'd come. The data analyst who'd felt invisible had become a published poet with a growing reputation. The defensive bookstore owner had evolved into a community facilitator who brought people together through shared love of stories.

"Any regrets, Mrs Jones?" Darius asked as they swayed together during the last dance of the evening.

"Only that we waited so long to stop analyzing our feelings and start trusting them," she replied, adjusting his tie with the familiarity of someone who'd be doing it for the rest of her life.

"Well, we have plenty of time to make up for it."

"All the time in the world."

As the reception wound down and they said goodbye to guests who'd traveled to celebrate with them, Danielle felt the profound satisfaction of a story that had reached its perfect beginning—because that's what this was, she realized. Not an ending, but the start of everything they'd been building toward.

They decided they would spend their honeymoon in Savannah, exploring bookstores and historic sites, writing letters to each other even though they'd be sharing a hotel room. They would return to Sweetgum to continue building their life together—expanding the bookstore's programming, supporting each other's writing careers, eventually talking about children and houses and all the ways their love could grow.

Later that night, in their hotel room overlooking Sweetgum's town square, they stood at the window watching the streetlights illuminate the quiet streets of the place that had brought them together.

"So," Danielle said, settling back against her husband's chest as his arms wrapped around her, "what's the first thing we write in our story as Mr and Mrs Jones?"

"That we choose each other," Darius replied, pressing a soft kiss to her temple. "Every day, for all the days we have left."

"I like that beginning."

"It's going to be a beautiful story."

And as they stood together looking out at the town that had watched their love story unfold, Danielle knew he was right. Because the best love stories, she'd learned, were the ones where two people found exactly what they needed in the person they least expected to understand them.

Theirs was going to be worth reading for a lifetime.

AUTHOR'S NOTE

Thank you so much for reading Dear Sweetgum, the fourteenth book in the Sweetgum Meadows Romance series of stand-alone novels. I really hope you loved it! If you enjoyed this book, please consider leaving a review so that others may also find it. Also, if you haven't read the first books yet, check them out today! Although these are stand-alone novels, the stories all intertwine and progress.

I look forward to introducing you to the other characters in this lovely, family-oriented town where each couple will find their happily ever after.

Would you like to receive bonus scenes and keep up with what's next with my upcoming books? Then, make sure you sign up for my mailing list on my website by visiting ImaniPrice.com.

ALSO BY IMANI PRICE

Book 1: Love Between Us

Book 2: Sweet Sunsets

Book 3: Infinite Kiss

Book 4: Dance With Me

Book 5: In Charge

Book 6: Forever With You

Book 7: Secret Sweethearts

Book 8: Endless Love

Book 9: The Harder We Fall

Book 10: Reservations of the Heart

Book 11: Play by Play

Book 12: Guarded Hearts

Book 13: Healing Hearts

Book 14: Dear Sweetgum

Book 15: Lanterns of the Meadows (novella)

Book 16: Drawn to You

Book 17: Under the Sweetgum Tree

Sweetgum Meadows' Visitor's Guide

My full audiobook catalog is available for FREE on YouTube. Check
it out here: https://swiy.co/Sweetgum

To all my lovely readers,

Thank you
for
reading